THE STORM

UNIVERSITY PRESS OF FLORIDA

Florida A&M University, Tallahassee
Florida Atlantic University, Boca Raton
Florida Gulf Coast University, Ft. Myers
Florida International University, Miami
Florida State University, Tallahassee
New College of Florida, Sarasota
University of Central Florida, Orlando
University of Florida, Gainesville
University of North Florida, Jacksonville
University of South Florida, Tampa
University of West Florida, Pensacola

The Storm

An Antebellum Tale of Key West

Ellen Brown Anderson

Edited by Keith L. Huneycutt

UNIVERSITY PRESS OF FLORIDA

Gainesville/Tallahassee/Tampa/Boca Raton
Pensacola/Orlando/Miami/Jacksonville/Ft. Myers/Sarasota

Cover: Depicting the Greenoughs' house from the perspective of the front entrance looking out across the porch, this pen-and-ink drawing was probably done by Mannevillette Brown or Georgia or Villette Anderson and was included with the manuscript. Courtesy of Jane and Raymond Gill and Elizabeth Traynor.

Copyright 2024 by Keith L. Huneycutt
All rights reserved
Published in the United States of America

29 28 27 26 25 24   6 5 4 3 2 1

Library of Congress Cataloging-in-Publication Data
Names: Anderson, Ellen Brown, 1814–1862, author. | Huneycutt, Keith L., 1956– editor.
Title: The storm : an antebellum tale of Key West / Ellen Brown Anderson ; edited by Keith L. Huneycutt.
Description: Gainesville : University Press of Florida, 2024. | Includes bibliographical references and index.
Identifiers: LCCN 2024012428 (print) | LCCN 2024012429 (ebook) | ISBN 9780813079141 (hardback) | ISBN 9780813070827 (pdf) | ISBN 9780813073439 (ebook)
Subjects: LCSH: Women pioneers—Florida—Key West—19th century—Fiction. | Key West (Fla.)—Social life and customs—19th century—Fiction. | LCGFT: Romance fiction. | Novellas.
Classification: LCC PS1039.A3655 S76 2024 (print) | LCC PS1039.A3655 (ebook) | DDC 813/.3—dc23/eng/20240326
LC record available at https://lccn.loc.gov/2024012428
LC ebook record available at https://lccn.loc.gov/2024012429

The University Press of Florida is the scholarly publishing agency for the State University System of Florida, comprising Florida A&M University, Florida Atlantic University, Florida Gulf Coast University, Florida International University, Florida State University, New College of Florida, University of Central Florida, University of Florida, University of North Florida, University of South Florida, and University of West Florida.

University Press of Florida
2046 NE Waldo Road
Suite 2100
Gainesville, FL 32609
http://upress.ufl.edu

To Marshi, Andrew and Jasmine, Sophia and Andrew

CONTENTS

List of Figures   ix
Acknowledgments   xi
Editorial Procedures and Policies   xiii

Introduction: Ellen Brown Anderson, Corinna Brown Aldrich, and Their Lives as Writers   1
Keith L. Huneycutt

The Storm   43

Afterword: An Editorial Note on the Manuscript; Attributing Authorship and Tracking the Manuscript's Path   85

Appendix A: Ellen Brown Anderson's "A Novel in a Nut-Shell"   95
Appendix B: Other Unpublished Manuscripts of Ellen Brown Anderson and Corinna Brown Aldrich   117
Appendix C: *The Storm*, True Womanhood, Feminism, and Companionate Marriage in Key West   121
Works Cited and Consulted   127
Index   135

FIGURES

1. Ellen Brown   xiv
2. Corinna Brown   xiv
3. Mannevillette Brown   2
4. James Anderson   7
5. Sketch of Key West, 1838   35
6. Daguerreotype of Key West, 1849   39
7. Engraving of wreckers at work   40
8. Photograph of Georgia Anderson   40
9. Photograph of Villette Anderson   41
10. Photograph of Ellen Brown Anderson, circa 1855   41
11. Photograph of the first page of *The Storm*   42
12. Drawing of mosquito tent   53
13. Drawing of perspective from the Greenoughs' house   69
14. Drawing of Jenny Greenough floating on flotsam   71

ACKNOWLEDGMENTS

I first want to express my gratitude to the descendants of Ellen Brown Anderson for their invaluable assistance, encouragement, and friendship as I worked on this project. For this book, Jane Gill and her husband, Raymond, have shared their family history, making it possible for me to understand how the manuscript of *The Storm* made its way from its likely place of origin to its current home at the University of Florida. Their niece, Elizabeth Traynor, has also provided multiple details of family history that filled in many gaps. Elizabeth, Jane, and Raymond also provided me with images of portraits of family members who probably had a hand in writing and illustrating *The Storm,* and they gave me permission to use all of the resources at their disposal.

Thanks go to Jim Cusick, curator of the P. K. Yonge Library of Florida History at the University of Florida, for drawing my attention to the manuscript of *The Storm* and then to Norm La Coe's essay and for sharing his knowledge and hospitality while I was in Gainesville. Without his help, this project never would have begun.

Special thanks go to the late Norm La Coe, who generously provided documented evidence concerning the provenance of the manuscript of *The Storm* between 1972 and 2015, provided his own insights and speculations about the authorship of *The Storm,* and kindly supported my efforts in this endeavor.

Many thanks go to James M. Denham, who has endlessly shared with me his encyclopedic knowledge of Florida history and resources and gave me encouragement and help throughout this project.

I would also like to thank Nora Galbraith, a recently retired interlibrary loan specialist at Florida Southern College's Roux Library, who could find anything, and Hillary Arieux, Roux Library's new resources sharing librarian, who helped me locate a number of items needed for my research. I would also like to thank Steven Wade, a former Roux Library information resources specialist, who used his impressive talent with electronic resources to help me.

 I also would like to thank the administration of Florida Southern College for granting me a sabbatical during the spring of 2021 to work on this book. I would like to thank Pete Schreffler, chair of the English Department at Florida Southern College, who helped me in numerous ways to make this project go smoothly. I would also like to thank the Department of English and Modern Languages' administrative assistant, Kathy Kniffin, who assisted me in transcribing the manuscript.

EDITORIAL PROCEDURES AND POLICIES

The manuscript for *The Storm* is in the archives of the P. K. Yonge Library of Florida History at the University of Florida, Gainesville, where I hope it has found its permanent home. I used a photocopy of this manuscript to transcribe the text with valuable assistance from Kathy Kniffin, the talented administrative assistant for the Department of English and Modern Languages at Florida Southern College, and I used digital photographs from the original manuscript for pages where any word or punctuation was in question. The editing of the text was relatively simple. The handwriting is generally neat and easy to read with few in-text corrections by the original writer or copyist. Other than the first page, which has some damage apparently caused by extended exposure to light, the manuscript is in good condition. Kathy Kniffin transcribed most of the text, and I transcribed the rest myself. I proofread the text multiple times and made corrections where needed.

As a general rule, I have retained original spellings and punctuation and provide annotations to clarify the author's diction or justify certain spellings. In a few instances, I have silently corrected obvious errors of the copyist, as when a word is doubled (i.e., "to to") at the end of one line and the beginning of the next or when part of a word is left out (i.e., "examing" instead of "examining"). The need for such corrections arose rarely.

Figure 1. Ellen Maria Brown at around age twenty. Miniature portrait painted by Mannevillette Brown. Courtesy of Jane and Raymond Gill and Elizabeth Traynor.

Figure 2. Corinna Brown at around age twenty-two. Portrait painted by Mannevillette Brown. Courtesy of Jane and Raymond Gill and Elizabeth Traynor.

Introduction

Ellen Brown Anderson, Corinna Brown Aldrich, and Their Lives as Writers

Keith L. Huneycutt

After *The Storm*, the ninety-page manuscript of an unpublished novella set in Key West, Florida, in the mid-nineteenth century, was donated to the P. K. Yonge Library of Florida History at the University of Florida in September 2015, it soon became apparent that the story had most likely been completed sometime between 1853 and 1862 by Ellen Brown Anderson. Her sister, Corinna Brown Aldrich, possibly collaborated with her between 1850 and 1853.

The absence of a name and a date on an unpublished manuscript naturally leads to questions about the story's provenance, but much evidence suggests that only these sisters could have written it, and further evidence suggests that it was all, or mostly, Ellen's. Because this manuscript can be tracked back from its current location at the University of Florida to its removal from a family storage chest containing these sisters' personal correspondence, other manuscripts of unpublished essays and stories, other family papers, and additional drafts of illustrations for *The Storm*, this tale must have been authored by someone in the family. Even more compelling evidence comes from the story of these sisters' lives: surviving correspondence between the sisters and other family members is the main source of knowledge about Corinna and Ellen. The extant collection of nineteenth-century and early-twentieth-century Anderson-Brown family papers includes around nine hundred letters. This collection, much of which has been published in recent years, is a rich source of information about what they did, thought, and felt and about their friends, family members, and experiences.[1] However, the picture of their lives is incomplete. There are no surviving letters *between* the sisters, presumably because they were so

Figure 3. Mannevillette Elihu Dearing Brown, self-portrait, age twenty-four. Courtesy of Jane and Raymond Gill and Elizabeth Traynor.

regularly together, living within close physical proximity to one another nearly their entire lives and often living in the same house, and it is not possible to know how many letters the sisters wrote that did not survive; they often mention letters that do not appear in the family collection. Still, much information about these sisters and their lives as writers is available.

The Brown sisters were born in Portsmouth, New Hampshire, Corinna in 1812 and Ellen in 1814, to Captain Elihu Dearing Brown (1777–1819) and Elizabeth Dearing Brown (1785–1832).[2] After their mother's death, the sisters remained in their Portsmouth home with their younger brothers, Charles (1816–1840) and George (1817–1857), and two aunts, Ann (?–1846) and Mary (?–1839). We know little about their childhoods and nothing about what kind of formal education, if any, they had. However, the earliest extant letter by either sister, Corinna's letter of January 31, 1832, to her older brother, Mannevillette (1810–1896), a successful young painter and lithographer then living in Philadelphia, reveals that twenty-year-old Corinna was already an accomplished letter writer. She complained that Ellen had taken her seat at the writing desk to send her own letter to Charles, who was currently living with Mannevillette.

During the next few years—before the sisters' migration to Florida—family letters show that the Brown sisters were very close to their family, especially their siblings and aunts. Their letters mostly share news about family and friends, discuss their finances and other business matters, and then offer their opinions on various topics. Their letters reveal that they read extensively and regularly quoted not only the Bible but also British authors such as William Shakespeare, Lord Byron, Edward Bulwar-Lytton, Charles Dickens, William Thackery, and Maria Edgeworth. They include words, phrases, and sentences from foreign languages, especially French, but also some Italian and, occasionally, Latin. The sisters—like their brothers who survived into adulthood—were lifelong learners. In one letter written on December 18, 1832, Corinna tells Mannevillette she is working to improve her French and that Ellen planned to teach Charles; later, when they move to Key West, the sisters start learning Spanish. Their adult education included other sorts of study also: while living in Philadelphia in 1834, they took Bible study classes and horseback riding lessons. The sisters, especially Ellen, loved dancing, so they attended both public and private balls in Philadelphia, as they did later in Florida, notably the military balls in St. Augustine. Though their opportunities were limited elsewhere, in Philadelphia the sisters attended many plays.

Working together from their Portsmouth home in 1833, Corinna and Ellen began collaborating on a novel by mail with Mannevillette, who had moved to Philadelphia in 1831. In a letter written on December 22, 1833, Corinna mentions to Mannevillette that she and Ellen had been thinking about his plan to make money by writing a book and asks him to send a detailed plan with the time of the story's setting and the specific location of the New England farm where it takes place. The next surviving letter, written two months later, jumps into the story's plot: "I forgot to say, George <u>must not</u> have a <u>sister</u>—you may give him anything but <u>kindred</u>. I believe I told you to introduce his father. We shaln't meddle with him until we get your part. Can't you make <u>his return</u> the means of <u>George's reform, somehow</u>? You may introduce anything or anybody that won't interfere with what <u>we</u> have written, but you see a sister would tare our part all to pieces,—Make George leave here in June; I said <u>May</u> before." On February 28, 1834, Corinna sent further plot details and instructions, adding, "I think we shall send you the first part of the book next week.... I have one request to make. Don't alter anything in it, excepting a misspelt word if there should be such a thing, ... lest it should affect the story. Send your part as soon as you can and make it <u>as long as you can</u>." By March

20, 1834, the book was finished, as Corinna wrote to Mannevillette: "We received all of your documents in due time and <u>arranged</u> them into our book!—but to speak plainly, Mann, we have not the least idea of its getting the prize, we have been altogether too much hurried about it, but we mean to do something yet.—our three heads. Yours was very good.—but we could not carry it fully into effect owing to the little time allowed us. But can't help it now. We shall probably forward it by Mr. Morris tomorrow, if not, I will send it your way." Shortly after receiving the book from his sisters, Mannevillette moved to Geneva, New York, to pursue new business opportunities, and on October 5, 1834, his sisters arrived with Charles in Philadelphia.

There, they would have found a vibrant cultural environment with a broad and deep literary history. How much they became directly involved in that culture during their ten months there is not completely clear, but they attended theater performances and balls and mixed with many people in polite society so that they were fully involved in the sophisticated world around them. These aspiring authors would have been keenly aware that the city was a center for book, magazine, and newspaper publishing. They might well have read copies of and met writers for publications such as *Graham's Magazine of Literature and Art* or the *American Quarterly Review*, which was, according to Ellis Oberholtzer, "a quarterly collection of high-minded essays upon political and literary topics" (194), or they might have encountered less high-minded material: "It was an age of low-priced newspapers and magazines filled with cheap, tawdry stories, sentimental poetry, puzzles, articles about the fashions of dress and cookery" (Oberholtzer 226). Among their many choices was the widely distributed *Saturday Evening Post* (226) and Louis A. Godey's *Lady's Book*, offering generally light "love stories and sentimental sketches . . . supplied by many writers, including . . . 'Grace Greenwood' (Mrs. Sarah J. Lippencott) [and] . . . Harriet Beecher Stowe"; it published writings by many established male writers also, including Edgar Allan Poe, who "contributed many stories, reviews and criticisms" (Oberholtzer 231).

Unfortunately, the three Brown siblings knew by autumn that their book had been rejected, and they had it back, revising it. In a letter to Mannevillette written on February 2, 1835, Corinna focuses on the process of attempting to publish the book, but she speaks of the book's authors as herself and Ellen and does not mention Mannevillette as having a part in it, suggesting that his role as an author was minor or that they might be working on a different book. This is also the first time Corinna has mentioned it as the first of two volumes and adds that in order to conceal their names and gender from the publishers, they used Charles as a go-between to deal with them:

> About our poor book, Mann, we finished the first volume, and thought it *pretty good,* and sent it to Carey and Lea. . . . They said they should like to keep it a week and look over it. That we agreed to; they did not know the authors [were] women. We told Charles to say it was sent to him, etc. They kept it a week and returned it, saying they could not publish it—whereupon we sent Charles round to see why & wherefore. Mr. Carey said it was written in a different style from the ordinary novel, and he did not know how it would take—that he did not like to give his opinion of it, but we must get some [other] human to read it and recommend it and then [page torn] it would sell, etc. Of course we could not do that so we laid it aside. We intend to send it to the Harpers; I think they would publish it . . . doubt if he read ten pages of it. He says he did not read it through. . . . I know if he had read it through he would have thought better of it. He says he thinks the author will make a fine writer. I should like to know how he arrived at that conclusion. He says we ought to write a while for periodicals, etc. . . . I am half inclined to take it elsewhere as it is, for I am confident Carey never read it, & would not have published it if it had been perfect.

The Brown sisters' choice to conceal their identities was typical for many writers of their time; as Johnathan Wells comments, "to be sure, many women writers struggled with the notion of revealing their identity in public and resorted to pseudonyms" (77). Despite their lack of publishing success, their time in Philadelphia was transformative for the Brown sisters. In this urbane environment, they encountered a wider range of people than they could have experienced in Portsmouth and were exposed to a vibrant, multifaceted literary culture. Corinna and Ellen left Philadelphia and returned to Portsmouth in July of 1835, and Corinna remarked in a July 4 letter to Mannevillette, "I wonder if I shall feel as I did when I left—I think not, in many respects—I think that I am . . . intellectually improved; that is, I have gained some knowledge of the world." There is no mention of the book during their four-month stay in Portsmouth, as their attention focuses on preparations for their upcoming move. Their ten months in Philadelphia prepared them for the much bigger changes in their lives that would come when they moved to Florida.

Finally, after their mother's estate was settled, they accepted the invitation from their Aunt Delia (?–1843) to move to her and her husband's Florida estate; Delia had moved to St. Augustine, East Florida, in 1832, established a millinery shop, and the next year married Dr. James Hall, a rich planter in Mandarin. Their older sister, Adelaide, had already moved in with Aunt Delia in Florida but died there late in 1832. Despite their sadness over the death of their sister, Corinna and Ellen moved in November 1835 to live with their aunts Mary and Ann, joining Charles, who had arrived in Mandarin two months before. Ellen described Mandarin to Mannevillette as "a place twelve miles from a village and forty from town in a flat sandy country, and such a flat sandy country would be Home" (Denham and Huneycutt 38). Charles remained there, but in 1837 Ellen went to St. Augustine to stay for the winter with the family of Judge Robert Reid, and Corinna moved to Jacksonville after marrying Dr. Edward Aldrich. The Aldriches moved frequently during the next few years—to Macon, Georgia, to St. Mary's, Georgia, to Mineral Springs, Florida, sometimes with Ellen coming along, and sometimes with Ellen going back to Mandarin. During this time, the sisters continued to send letters to Mannevillette, who had in 1838 moved to Paris, France, to study art, copy masterworks, and paint portraits for a living. No doubt Mann, as they called him, was always happy to receive their lengthy letters, but no doubt the contents sometimes worried him. In a letter written on January 12, 1836, to Mannevillette, Ellen comments on the mix of people in the surrounding region: "The society here is as yours, a mixture of the poor genteel and the rich vulgar as you could imagine—the rich who belong here and own negroes and lands and the poor who have come here in hopes of getting them, all hopes, however are deferred on account of the war with the Seminoles. . . . You don't know how striking the contrast is to be between living here and in Phila. I feel as if I was out of the world. . . . Here . . . an Aaron's serpent (Exodus 7:8–13) in the shape of this Indian war has swallowed up every other subject of interest. Every day brings new reports, and each more interesting than the last" (Denham and Huneycutt 20–21). This letter from Corinna, written on July 12, 1836, might well have alarmed Mannevillette: "Creeks and Seminoles . . . [might] unite. . . . I think a more bloody and ruinous war will be fought with these savages before they are subdued, than has ever yet been witnessed on our fair land. The accounts of the Creek Indians' deeds of horror are enough to curdle our own heart's blood. . . . I say Mann, what a pretty fix the country would have been in if we had gone to war with France! Or even should the slaves rise about this time, it would

Figure 4. Lt. James Willoughby Anderson, daguerreotype taken just after the siege of Vera Cruz, Mexico, 1846. Courtesy of Jane and Raymond Gill and Elizabeth Traynor.

make a glorious work—the horrors of St. Domingo enacted over again in earnest" (Denham and Huneycutt 21–23). And yet, in the very next sentence, Corinna switches the scene to suggest that all is indeed well: "Mr. David Levy of St. Augustin is here today, he is playing chess with Ell. I say this that you may know we are pretty generally quiet" (22–23). Perhaps the most notable thing about the Brown sisters' new circumstances living in territorial Florida is not the cultural difference between the sophisticated Northeast and the much rougher Florida frontier, or even the very real danger from the Second Seminole War flaring up around them; instead, the real surprise is how well the sisters adjusted to these circumstances. In a letter of May 25, 1836, Corinna shares the most recent news with Mannevillette and tells him that everyone wants Ellen and her to leave Mandarin for the comparative safety of Jacksonville, but, she says, "we laugh at them. I deem no part of the Territory less liable to attack than another, and again I would almost as lief encounter the Indians as the Jacksonville mob. It is the nastyest dirtyest place I ever was in & such a hole as you never saw." After she tells him that they enjoy laughing at the locals during the hubbub of false alarms, she adds, "this leaves all well & in good spirits.... If there is danger, we shall get off—so don't be alarmed. We shall put our cowardly legs in requisition quicker!" (Denham and Huneycutt 27–28).

The Brown sisters' letters frequently discuss their worries regarding Seminole raids, but they do not display much interest in the lives of the Indigenous people. They almost certainly would have disagreed with anti-removal activists from the northern states they had left behind; since both sisters were married to men directly involved with the U.S. Army's mission to remove the Seminoles from Florida, they probably strongly supported the 1830 Indian Removal Act. Although their letters sometimes praised the courage, cleverness, and determination of the Seminole and Creek warriors, like the other white settlers and U.S. soldiers around them, they referred to Indigenous people as "savages."

Late in 1839, Edward, Corinna, and Ellen moved to Newnansville, the biggest inland town in East Florida and the heavily fortified center for U.S. military forces fighting the Seminoles. Edward served there as surgeon and planned to establish a private practice. The isolated log cabin town, around seventy difficult miles from Mandarin, was about as distant culturally from the Northeast as one could imagine. In a letter written December 14, 1839, Ellen described their new home: "After I have written log-house, pine tree, and cracker the only addition I can summon to memory is pig and dog. You mix up these ingredients ... add a little of some proportion of alcohol and the result will always be Newnansville" (Denham and Huneycutt 105). Dreary as the place seemed to Corinna and Ellen, the town was relatively safe, with four army posts surrounding it, and the presence of U.S. soldiers in the town itself added further security and even social opportunities. Ellen soon found herself courted by Lt. James Anderson and married him on October 26, 1840. Although she remained close to the Aldriches, when James's duties took him elsewhere, such as St. Augustine or Palatka, she went too. Eventually, they had three children: Edward Willoughby, 1841–1915; Corinna Georgia (Georgia), 1843–1874; and Ellen Mannevillette (Villette), 1847–1891. In 1844, when James was shipped off with his regiment to fight in the war with Mexico, Ellen and their children moved with Edward and Corinna to Pensacola. There, she received the news of James's death in September 1847. Although Ellen would receive a widow's pension from the U.S. government, she relied on support from her brothers Mannevillette and George, and she lived with the Aldriches for the next several years as they moved to Macon, Georgia, then Marietta, and in June 1849, to Key West, Florida.

As they moved from place to place, Ellen and Corinna continued to correspond with Mannevillette about their writing projects and further attempts at publication. The sisters left behind a number of manuscripts, including several stories and fragments, which have been passed down through their descendants and remain in the possession of family members. Corinna apparently refers to one of these stories in an August 1836 letter to Mannevillette, now living in Ithaca, New York, which reveals that the sisters had begun working on a new novel:

> Nab [Ellen] and I are writing a book—I think it will be pretty good! We shall have it done about the first of November, but how shall we get it to you and what will you do with it? We can send it to NY. Is there anyone I can direct it to who will forward it to you? If we send it—you must get it published if you can get anyone to buy it—better try the Harpers. Let them submit it to a committee if they choose, but on no account give up our names! It will be a sort of take off and would make us liable to severe remarks . . . swear not to say who wrote it—for we have hit up two or three I am afraid will know their pictures as it is. (Denham and Huneycutt 44)

The book was planned as a social satire, evidently targeting the Northern society that they had left behind for Florida. Unfortunately, as they explained to Mannevillette in a letter written on November 2, they had to abandon the project to take care of Dr. Hall and Aunt Ann. However, a partial draft that might be the first chapter of this story remains in the family collection. This seventeen-page manuscript, titled *Sketches of Life During the Second Seminole War*, consists of a single chapter subtitled "The Elopement." Set in Portsmouth, New Hampshire (the Browns' hometown), in 1831, the story begins as Alice, the spoiled and naive seventeen-year-old daughter of Colonel and Mrs. Garland, elopes with the rascally Captain Conrad to New York City. The story breaks off here, so the reader never learns what the authors had planned for this couple when they get to Florida or what happens to them during the Seminole War (76).[3] The fragment's title, however, suggests that the Brown sisters recognized the opportunities that Florida offered for fiction and that they hoped to incorporate their personal experiences of this conflict into a literary creation. As in several other Brown sister stories and fragments, the protagonist is a young girl entering the larger social world beyond her family, and as in *The Storm*, she faces that world married at a very young age. This fragment resembles *The Storm* in other aspects, such as opening with epigraphs consisting of poetry quoted from a famous author—lines from William Cooper to begin *The Storm* and for this story fragment, Lord Byron. Both pieces include frequent moralizing narrative commentary, as in this passage from *Sketches:*

> Strange it may appear that an intelligent and affectionate mother should thus have reared a daughter, it is nevertheless true. But she was the eldest, and for a long time the only child; yet it is a lamentable fact, that too many of our young ladies of the present day, of far less wealth, are educated with no more reference to their becoming wives and mothers, than if their ambitious progenitors had not that end in view and with even less reference to the probable vicissitudes of our fortunes changing hands; as if such mutations as daily occur were not only improbable, but impossible; as if a mother's love could will all she wishes; could in afterlife, with God-like powers shield the darling of her heart from all the storms of future life, even as her mantle in infancy may protect it from the wind and rain! Would to God it could; for what love so sincere, so endless, so nearly allied to Divinity? (16–17)

This passage also displays the concern with the education of girls that Ellen often expressed in her letters—and that appears prominently in *The Storm*. Another similarity is the author's frequent use of figurative language and her particular fondness for nautical and weather metaphors, many involving storms, as in the final paragraph of *Sketches*: "She had launched upon an unknown sea; and that without chart or compass; but Innocence stands at the helm. May Providence guide the way. We herewith transcribe the calms and storms of her perilous voyage through life" (*Sketches* 17). For comparison, here is one excerpt from *The Storm:*

> There are great storms in life, when we are borne through deep waters, helpless yet safe in the ark of our innocence. When we emerge therefrom into new scenes and circumstances, the recollection of these former events recedes in imagination, until they seem part of a former existence. Such are the pictures which now rush on my memory, as I look back upon the long past. But I cannot let you see it all. Words have painted for you my house and my garden, words shall tell you of my friends, and my home, but no words can paint the storm which arose in my soul,—the cloud no bigger than a man's hand, which overspread the whole sky of my life, and ended in one terrific storm. (52–53)

There is no more mention of this unfinished novel, but in a letter of June 6, 1837, Corinna tells Mann that she hopes to win $100 in prize money entering a Philadelphia writing contest—and win she did. However, as her letter of July 5, 1837, explains,

> As for those impudent Editors of the Chronicle—they awarded me the prize and payed me what? Ten dollars instead of one hundred. I sent them a letter—under my assumed name. I am sure they have swindled me—if the tale was not worth one hundred dollars, it was not the prize tale and ought not to have been published as such. I jawed them well. And I will give them more of the same if they will give me a chance—good thing they don't know who they are fighting with. I will have my fun, if I can't get my pay. I know the trash is not worth one hundred dollars—but that is not the thing—they promised to pay that for the best offered—& if that was the best I ought to have it. Don't let on that I am the author of "The Grumble Family." For the world I would not have it known. Is it ill or well received? Have the other papers copied it?

Corinna's piece, "The Grumble Family: A Tale of Modern Times," appeared in the June 3, 1837, issue of the *Philadelphia Saturday Chronicle*. The piece illustrates the difference between the styles of Corinna's creative work and Ellen's. Corinna's story is light and generally funny, and the characters are undeveloped caricatures: the boisterous, drunken Esquire Grumble is intimidated by his strong-willed wife; his three oldest daughters are lazy and ignorant, and they all marry rich, shallow men. Mary, the youngest daughter, a Cinderella figure, works hard and tries to maintain the household. The tale's narrator, Glue Simpson, waits until he makes his fortune to rescue her from her parents, who have lost their money due to foolish investments. Corinna's story lacks the long, moralizing narrative passages that Ellen favored; it uses little figurative language; the transitions are often abrupt or missing; and in general, though it is entertaining, it is less polished than Ellen's stories.

The next discussion of professional writing comes in a joint letter from the sisters to Mannevillette on December 21, 1837. Ellen tells Mann that their friend Reverend David Brown had become the editor of the Jacksonville *Courier*, and she has "promised to drop a penful of ink for him occasionally" (Denham and Huneycutt 69). On January 17, Corinna wrote that Reverend Brown was visiting: "I promised to write for him but somehow I can't find time to answer the demands of my private correspondence &

business—to write public documents. Ell favoured him with an address for the New Year—but it was thought too severe—and only part of it was published" (Denham and Huneycutt 72). A month later, Ellen wrote, "I have written an article for a new magazine that is to be forthcoming in March—to be published by Parson Brown and called *The Florida Magazine* . . . I wrote it for the *Courier* but he begged it for the magazine which I take to be something of a compliment although it may not be so but merely taken to fill up the book" (Denham and Huneycutt 74). Unfortunately, the magazine was never published, and this is the last reference for a dozen years in either sister's letters to any desire or attempt to write fiction or essays. Their mostly bad experience with the publishing world was probably one reason, but many other factors must have contributed: the sisters and their husbands moved almost constantly from place to place, and sometimes they were in isolated places where settling in was difficult—and whenever they were settled enough to write, they spent much of their time writing lengthy, detailed letters. No doubt the stress of living in remote, rustic locations—not to mention the strain of living in an active war zone with the threat of physical danger—added to their limited writing activity. Ellen was also busy, and at times overwhelmed, raising her children. Although James was apparently a good father, he was frequently absent on military duty and wasn't much help. His death in Mexico in 1847 left her to raise three children alone with the prospect of living on a small widow's pension. Corinna loved the children, but her and Edward's frequent moves often meant that she was unavailable to help, and the deaths of Aunt Mary in 1839 and Aunt Ann in 1846, along with Ellen's estrangement from Aunt Delia, meant that she had little to no family childrearing support. She was dedicated to this task, but she expressed in her letters the frustration of having little time to herself.

For Edward, Corinna, and Ellen, the move to Key West in May 1849 took them to a new world. Although isolated from the rest of Florida, Key West presented many more socializing opportunities than any place they had lived in since St. Augustine, and the interesting ethnic and cultural mixture, along with the exciting business of the place, gave them a great deal to write about in their letters. Their spirits seemed to improve, and during their time there, the sisters wrote some of their best letters, with precise descriptions of the island's natural beauty, keen observations on the residents, commentary on the activities around them, and disquisitions on topics such as marriage, food, politics, art, and their personal lives.

Key West stimulated Ellen's drive to write and publish. Several months after their arrival, she wrote to Mannevillette, "Have you ever read *Vanity Fair*? Do you remember how we tried to get it in New York? Well, we borrowed it here, and a very entertaining book it is, containing some most accurate likenesses of 'humans' as the Florida crackers say. I have a great mind to undertake a *Vanity Fair* in America. I think I could do it. If I only had a study all to myself, and if and but, and if, and but, and if, and but, and so on" (Denham and Huneycutt 261–62). The sisters left Florida for good in May 1850, moving to New York City and then to Bridgeport, Connecticut, for several months. Ellen remained serious about writing and did in fact anonymously publish "A Novel in a Nut-Shell" in the September 1850 issue of the *Knickerbocker*. (See appendix A for the story in its entirety.)

Apparently, Corinna no longer shared Ellen's aspiration for a writing career. In the past, Corinna seemed to take the lead on joint creative projects and had succeeded at least in publishing a story. But the cumulative effect of living an unstable existence fueled by Edward's restless peregrinations—moving from place to place, never satisfied with his medical practice—had perhaps taken something out of her. Edward failed to gain the position as military surgeon in Key West, so he left for San Francisco in the midst of the gold rush to establish a private practice, and though he maintained regular correspondence with the family, Corinna never saw him again. While Edward attempted to set up his business, Corinna planned to join him in California and for Ellen and the children to go with her. Ellen, however, declared to Mannevillette in a letter of October 18, 1850, "I will go only . . . if I can get there something to do whereby I can maintain myself . . . But could or can I get anything I can do there or elsewhere, I shall not be slow in improving the opportunity." From Bridgeport, the sisters moved back to New York City in November 1850, visited Newnansville and Liberty Bluff, Florida, to attend George's wedding in early 1851, then returned to New York in July, after which their living situation became increasingly unstable. During the next six months, they lived at five different boardinghouses in New York City. By December 1853, the relationship between the sisters had become strained. In a letter of February 15, 1854, Edward wrote to Mannevillette explaining that he could not allow Corinna to journey to California because "she would disgrace herself, & perhaps die on the way, for in those packet steamers, rum flows as freely as water, and the women generally drink as much as the men. . . . There is one habit which she has been addicted to for years, that of taking one or two doses daily of Morphine—Were she placed under any kind of restraint, it would be wrong & impossible to withhold that from her, except at the expense of her life" (Denham and Huneycutt 283–84).

In a letter of June 5, 1854, Ellen wrote to Mannevillette that Corinna "is quite regular in her habits . . . if there is any change, it is not for the better. . . . It is a great blessing to me that you and George have undertaken to take care of me. My situation would now be dreadful and I should be driven to some desperate measures to rid myself of the indignity and insult I should have to suffer if you had not put it in my power to be independent of Corinna." Corinna's condition continued to worsen, and the family finally committed her to the Bloomingdale Asylum, where she died on November 30, 1854. The next few years were especially bleak for Ellen. She lived in several different boarding houses, suffered from constant financial strain, and worried constantly about her children's welfare. Her brothers sent money when possible, though neither could give her as much as they wanted. Still, Ellen managed to tutor her children, to enroll the girls in school at half price, and to send Edward to free public school. To help pay her expenses, she took in boarders, but she frequently had to endure unpleasant disputes with them, and because of her poor health, she had to hire a servant to help with the housework. When George died in October 1857, that source of income for Ellen was cut off, though in 1859, Ellen's military pension was increased to $300. Furthermore, she developed a close relationship with J. Egbert Farnum, a notorious character who had served in the Mexican war, engaged in filibustering expeditions, and later was incarcerated for piracy. Farnum, who wrote numerous letters to Ellen between 1858 and 1860 and seems to have been very close to her and her children, might have provided financial support.

Nevertheless, Ellen was determined to become independent, and she believed that she could best support herself by writing. In a letter of December 13, 1857, Ellen tells Mannevillette that she is still considering writing for a living and recounts her past efforts at writing, adding that she has had article manuscripts stolen and plagiarized. Despite her health issues and domestic responsibilities, Ellen made a go of it, and she explains to Mannevillette in a letter written on September 4, 1859, that she was reading the proof sheets and writing a review of a novel, *Beulah*, "by a southern lady, Miss Evans," adding that she had taken the job with no compensation.[4] It was arranged by Farnum, she said, and might lead to other jobs.

The Composition of *The Storm*

The Storm could have been started as early as late May or early June 1849, when the sisters arrived in Key West, and Corinna might have worked with Ellen in the early composition stage. However, Corinna's health was already declining, and none of her letters in recent years had mentioned writing. Corinna departed for New York around October 23 and returned to Key West five months later, apparently to help prepare for the entire family's departure from the island. Unfortunately, there are no surviving letters from Corinna or Ellen written during these five months and therefore no record of what Ellen did during Corinna's absence. Whether she started working on the story then or later is unclear, but it seems likely that Ellen did most or all of the writing and finished it after Corinna's death. One piece of evidence supporting this assumption is a narrative reference on page 34 of *The Storm* to Mrs. Potiphar, a character in George William Curtis's *The Potiphar Papers*, published in 1853. If Corinna did have a hand in the story, she probably could not have maintained involvement through the story's completion, since she was unlikely to have read Curtis's book before she died in November 1854 due to her grave condition and confinement in the asylum.[5]

The Storm's plot and setting point to an author with precisely the background and experiences of the Brown sisters. The descriptions in the story of the island's flora, houses and other buildings, and overall community resemble the sisters' descriptions of Key West in their letters. The narrator's grumbling about mosquitoes sounds a great deal like the constant complaints in the sisters' letters about these pests. In the surviving Key West letters—twelve by Ellen and ten by Corinna—mosquito complaints arise often. One reference in *The Storm* is especially suggestive: "The writer of this history has known an army to be turned back by them, and military operations delayed for defenses against them, in Florida,—and not without reason" (13). Having arrived in Florida at the outset of the Second Seminole War and living close to the conflict until its termination in 1842, Corinna and Ellen were quite familiar with the operations—and difficulties—of the U.S. Army in Florida.

The Storm's narrator, Jenny Greenough, explains that she married at sixteen and moved from New York to Key West with her husband, Peter, a twenty-nine-year-old physician whose purpose for moving to Key West was to make a fortune. Corinna was in fact married to a physician, Edward

Aldrich, who moved to Key West hoping to secure a comfortable government post at the marine hospital and open a private practice. In the story, Jenny's sister, Malinda, and her husband also move to the island, and they soon move in with the Greenoughs. Similarly, while on the island, Corinna and Ellen lived together, as they did for most of their lives.

The Storm is set in Key West at an unspecified time, but the main event of the story, a destructive and deadly storm, is undoubtedly based on the hurricane that struck the Keys in October 1846, destroyed most of the island's structures, and killed at least sixty of the fifteen hundred residents, a major disaster that the author of *The Storm* could have learned a good deal about from reports appearing in newspapers. Ellen and Corinna commented on this catastrophe in their correspondence even before they moved to Key West.[6] Later, in a letter written on June 21, 1849, to Mannevillette, Corinna remarks, "If it were not for the dread of the hurricane, I think [the residents] would make a beautiful place—but they are wholly discouraged since the storm of 46 that destroyed all the gardens—indeed it laid waste the city—blew down houses—uprooted trees—and made havoc everywhere—But the house we live in withstood the gale" (Denham and Huneycutt 244). Similarly, in a letter written on July 26, Ellen observes that the island had few living trees, yet "There are a good many dead ones, but they are not large. I fancy they have been killed by the gale" (Denham and Huneycutt 250). While they lived on the island, Corinna and Ellen were ideally situated to hear firsthand accounts from surviving witnesses and to see for themselves the long-term damage to vegetation and structures. The consequences of the 1846 storm were still visible everywhere on the island, and memories of the event remained fresh in people's minds.

The Storm is full of specific observations about Key West shipwreck salvaging, a thriving industry at mid-century.[7] The story's narrator provides abundant, detailed information about the wrecking business and expresses great admiration for the wreckers. For instance, this passage appears on page 13 of the story: "The little vessels float over those dangerous waters, like white winged angels of mercy, and make us indignant that such should have been associated with the hateful name of pirate."

Both sisters mention visiting a wrecker's observation cupula in June 1849 at about the time they visited the island's lighthouse, a sturdier structure built to replace the one destroyed by the 1846 storm, and Ellen discusses the business in several other letters. In a letter to Mannevillette written on October 23, 1849, she provides this account praising wreckers and wrecking:

I wonder what your idea of a wrecker is! A piratical sort of fellow, whiskers and beard outside, and rascality in? Is that it? ... La me! They are ... like men everywhere else. Some are liberal, others stingy. ... they live in comfortable houses, grumble about expenses, and pursue their avocations in as business-like a manner as any shopkeeper you could find, the rascality being with the one as with the other, in the counting room, not upon the sea. Upon the sea, they are the ablest of seamen; necessarily so: for it is their business, in calm and storm, to go to the relief of distressed vessels, and their arrangements for this purpose are as business-like and systematic as those of any other trade or calling and a wrecker may be as honest and as honorable a man as any other, and yet not have to quit his trade for conscience' sake. (Denham and Huneycutt 275–76)

Much as the narrator of *The Storm* extols the noble character of the wreckers, Ellen praises not only their skill and brave deeds but also their honorable nature. Perhaps Ellen wanted to counteract the unsavory reputation that these shipwreck salvagers had once held with some justification in order to reassure her brother that she was living in a safe, pirate-free community. As Dorothy Dodd explains, the profession originated with the remnants of the fierce Calusa tribe that preyed upon wrecked and stranded vessels until the remaining Calusas moved to Cuba with the Spanish in 1763 after the Treaty of Paris turned Florida over to the British. The Calusas were soon followed by unscrupulous turtlers and fishers from the Bahamas in the eighteenth century (Dodd 175). Nevertheless, by the time the story was written, as Dodd makes clear, "wrecking was a well-organized, systematic, and legal business" (175). *The Storm*'s narrator displays extensive nautical knowledge, which would be natural for Corinna and Ellen, who spent a good deal of time on ships themselves, grew up in a port city, and came from a family whose living came from their father's profits as captain of a privateering vessel, *The Fox*. Although Ellen would have been five years old and Corinna seven at the death of their father,[8] they probably remembered him well. As they grew older, the sisters no doubt heard tales of his exploits and realized that, although it was lucrative and daring, privateering was a somewhat shady business. Nevertheless, as adults, they would have been predisposed to think the best of brave seamen, including privateers and wreckers.

Many details in *The Storm* particular to wrecking operations could have come from sources such as newspaper stories, court records, conversations with island residents, and interviews with the wreckers themselves. However, most published accounts of wrecking focused on the ships in action on the sea, and court records dealt with the legal claims on the salvaged goods. In contrast, most passages that mention wrecking in *The Storm* concern the direct impact of the business on the island's families and the methods used to facilitate the purchase of salvaged goods by the residents—a more domestic emphasis natural to someone who had personally examined these goods out of curiosity and in search of bargains for herself and her family, an activity that in the mid-nineteenth century would have been more likely carried out by women than men. Corinna and Ellen were perfectly positioned to gain firsthand knowledge of the distribution of products salvaged from wrecked ships.

In a letter written less than a month after arriving in Key West, Ellen already shows a keen interest in the fate of these goods:

> I expect the constant wrecking brings a great many curious things to this place. The other day, we were shown a great number of statuettes, as they are called, little statues three or four inches high, illustrative of the Mexican people and customs. They belonged to the French minister, who was taking them home; the vessel he was on board was wrecked, and they, with the other cargo, had to be sold to pay salvage. I could not help feeling sorry for the poor fellow, who had to lose them. If giving any person a vivid idea is proof of the skill of an artist, these were the work of no ordinary hand, for they were the most life-like things I ever saw. They were executed in wax, and colored to resemble life. (Denham and Huneycutt 247)

Most significantly, the tone and opinions about women's societal roles expressed in Jenny Greenough's narrative closely follow those of Ellen. *The Storm* presents a skeptical view of marriage, especially for young women, and expresses indignation over women's subordinate status in a patriarchal society. Jenny Greenough laments that she has been prepared for no role in life other than that of wife: her parents, she says, "in conjunction with the rest of the world, believed that a young woman was born, destined, foreordained, and commissioned to get married" (4). She adds, "That a young woman should be properly qualified to superintend a kitchen, and keep a house, was in the estimation of my mother, the only preparation necessary to fit her to be married. I was thought to be well educated" (26–27). Her discontent over her confined position as a married woman often takes on a feminist tone.[9] Elsewhere, Jenny complains openly about the education offered to girls; for example, when she is engaged in a dialogue with Mr. Mansfield, the lighthouse keeper, she tells him, "It seems to me, we women never have a chance to mature.... It is the fashion to take us from school at sixteen and seventeen, and set us about getting married, whereas boys of the same age are put at school, trade, or business, and the hardest kind of study." She adds, "I wish I had been a different person" (53). When Philip Mansfield, the lighthouse keeper's son, asks her, "Why don't you read?" She remains silent, but Jenny's narrative voice responds, "I did read. It seemed to me that reading did not answer the purpose" (53). Peter, Jenny's husband, compounds her unhappiness by dismissing her interests and concerns and with his condescension toward her lack of sophistication.

Throughout the Brown sisters' letters to and from their brothers, lively discussions about marriage frequently arise: the sisters engage in a long-term epistolary debate with Mannevillette about the proper or ideal marriage, taking care to educate him from the perspective of women. They frequently offer advice to him and to George, urging their brothers to consider carefully before making a commitment and, when they do, to marry intelligent women. Corinna and Ellen both married decent, well-educated men who apparently loved them and treated them well. However, Ellen, who married at age twenty-five and was widowed at thirty-two with three young children to care for, was dismayed over her inability to provide for herself and for them. In a letter to Mannevillette written on September 3, 1849, from Key West, she exclaims,

> Bless my stars what a helpless individual a woman is! What a ninny she can be. If it was not wicked I would wish myself a man. I would put my two legs into a pair of trousers and take the longest kind of steps, I don't know where. The fact is . . . a woman, having children, not having money, not having youth, beauty, or fascinations is a nuisance . . . a blot, and a nastiness in creation, and such is your . . . sister. (Denham and Huneycutt 268)

Ellen was probably familiar with the feminist ideas that had recently come out of the Seneca Falls Convention, led by Elizabeth Cady Stanton and Lucretia Mott in 1848 in Seneca Falls, New York, which produced "The Declaration of Sentiments" concerning women's rights, and with the first National Women's Rights Convention, organized by Lucy Stone in 1850 in Worcester, Massachusetts. While other important American and British authors championed equal rights for women before *The Storm* was written, British author Mary Wollstonecraft was perhaps the most significant. Ellen, who read a wide variety of American and British authors, would probably have been familiar with her writings. Wollstonecraft argued in her 1792 *A Vindication of the Rights of Woman* that women are rational creatures and should be educated as such. Wollstonecraft lamented "the neglected education of my fellow-creatures" (Wollstonecraft 29). As one critic puts it, "Wollstonecraft criticized the social system which limited women by encouraging them to nurture vanities and frivolities, thus preventing them from developing either their minds or their moral capabilities" (Benstock 52). In *The Storm*, Jenny Greenough's moral capabilities seem secure, but two other women in this story are deficient in that area, both the worldly, charming, flirtatious, and perhaps adulterous Mrs. Cantwell and Malinda, Jenny's even more charming, beautiful, and certainly adulterous sister. These women have no formal education, and clearly their morals are untrained—exactly the kind of women that Wollstonecraft scorned, on the one hand, but hoped to see improved by education, on the other. She believed that the minds of women "are not in a healthy state . . . that strength and usefulness are sacrificed to beauty," which she attributed to "a false system of education" (Wollstonecraft 29).

Ellen's surviving letters comment in a frustrated voice on the poor education, training, and opportunities available for women. When discussing these same topics, Jenny Greenough in *The Storm* sounds very much like Ellen Anderson.

The Storm and Literary Culture

For much of their adult lives, Corinna and Ellen aspired to be writers, and this was a realistic goal. American literary culture boomed during the antebellum years. According to Karen Manners Smith, "In the forty years preceding the Civil War, advances in printing technology and the unprecedented national growth of literacy produced an American reading public hungry for fiction and a publishing industry—authors, editors, publishers, and booksellers—eager to satisfy the new demand" (48). Moreover, women were increasingly entering the market to help fulfill this demand. As Thadious M. Davis explains, "Because of the limited opportunities for female wage earners, the new market for books and the possibility of a decent livelihood spurred women into authorship" (22). Corinna and Ellen eagerly entered writing contests for prize money, but for Ellen, after her time in Key West, she saw writing as an attainable career.

That the Brown sisters were members of this reading public is certain;

what exactly they read—and could have influenced their own writing goals—is less certain, but their letters do mention many books and authors. Most of those books were by men, yet they might have mentioned other works in letters that are now lost. And since most of their surviving letters are to their male relatives, they might have hesitated to mention books by women, perhaps thinking that the men might not take those—or them—seriously. Still, it seems safe to assume that they were familiar with more books than they mention in these letters, and some were probably bestsellers by women. To what degree *The Storm* was influenced by or reacted to these books is unknowable. Still, it is useful to survey major trends in writing by women in the antebellum United States in order to consider where *The Storm* fits in. Although the Brown sisters lived in the South for fifteen years and often had limited access to new books, magazines, and newspapers, as Jonathan Daniel Wells points out, "Southern women read the same authors that were highly regarded in the North" (60).[10] They visited larger cities, such as Charleston, with bookstores, but Ellen and Corinna often lived far from bookstores, so they borrowed books when they could or had them mailed to them through the surprisingly reliable postal system. Their letters mention periodicals much less often than books, but magazines and newspapers were clearly available. And although Ellen and Corinna were sometimes constrained by their limited budgets, periodicals were generally inexpensive, as Wells makes clear (62). Their letters reveal that they kept up with regional and national news, and they knew publications and publishers where they could submit their own writings. Despite their distance from publishing centers, the sisters participated in the vibrant print culture of the antebellum United States.

One especially important genre within antebellum literary culture was travel literature. Susan Roberson notes, "With advances in transportation technology not only could travelers make a voyage more quickly and cheaply to vacation spots like Niagara, but they could more ably move the nation further westward in a linear progression that seemed to many to be providential." She adds that a "national 'narrative of progress' . . . informed much of the rhetoric of antebellum America" (1). Roberson lists many classic male writers, such as Emerson, Whitman, Thoreau, and James Fenimore Cooper, whose writings exemplify the "geo-progressive narrative" of the day (1–2). Roberson adds that women writers also wrote texts that included them in this literature of "Manifest Destiny." Commenting on an 1845 travel sketch in *Godey's Lady's Book* by "Miss Leslie," Roberson explains,

Eliza Leslie positions herself and other women in the stories of American travel and the narratives of nation that were current in the Antebellum period, reminding readers that women too were out on the public road.... [W]omen were claiming their share of American mobilities as they traveled, moved, relocated, migrated, escaped from enslavement, and as they wrote about mobility in their novels, autobiographies, diaries, periodical essays, and travel books. (2–3)

Ellen and Corinna certainly took part in this national narrative with the epistolary accounts of their travels in the expanding Florida frontier. In *The Storm*, Ellen enters the travel narrative genre with her depiction of life in America's southernmost town, Key West, along with narratives of steamboat travel down the East Coast from New York to Florida and back, including a dramatic steamboat disaster and a catastrophic storm. Few writers in her day recognized the literary potential of this southern frontier as a contributor to the national travel genre. Cooper is a notable exception, though his story, like those of most other antebellum Key West writers, is infused with only secondhand details; of the women writers using the Keys in their fiction, only Ellen had direct experience of the island.

Roberson adds, "This national narrative that set its people afoot in the name of commerce competed with a narrative of domesticity that emerged as an answer to the unsettling of society in the early decades of the nineteenth century" (3–4). Commerce was in fact the reason for Jenny's adventures in Key West; like many other men, Peter was lured there to make a quick fortune, and along with the greed that drives him is his insistence that Jenny remain confined in her domestic sphere. Roberson says that "For some women, travel illustrated the freedom of movement and the expansion of knowledge and power that are often associated with it" (4). Ellen's tale completes this pattern: when fate delivers Jenny from her stifling marriage to Peter, she chooses a second marriage that allows her to enjoy the full benefits of travel and knowledge.

The Brown sisters probably read and were influenced by much of the rich and varied antebellum literature written for and by women. According to Joyce W. Warren, many nineteenth-century women writers "were widely read in their day. In fact, all of the bestsellers in the mid-nineteenth century were by women" (1). *The Storm* resists comfortable placement into any single category, but it shares traits with works representing several contemporary categories, even those that Warren calls "seduction novels," since this group provides examples of early works with a woman at the center, such as Susanna Rowson's *Charlotte Temple* (1794) and Hannah Foster's *The Coquette* (1797). "*The Coquette*, particularly," explains Warren, "thanks to the author's careful portrayal of the dilemma of [Eliza Wharton's] circumscribed situation and the poverty of her choices within American society, provides a provocative comment on the ideology of the dominant culture, which prescribes simply that the character should marry as soon as possible" (5). These words equally describe Jenny Greenough's situation in *The Storm*.

Joanne Dobson emphasizes the importance of nineteenth-century women's works in realism:

> From the start, female realists were concerned with the attempt to portray with verisimilitude the American landscape and the dynamics of American community. By mid-century, Susan Warner, Harriet Beecher Stowe, and Alice Cary excelled at representing the commonplace rhythms of daily life in a specific place at a specific time: rural New England, the antebellum South, the developing frontier. (172)

Ellen Brown Anderson provides a similarly realistic look at Key West with details about domestic and community life from a woman's perspective, which had never been attempted before.

A broad, widespread category of women's writing is embodied in the term "sentimental," which, Warren points out, was once a neutral word but grew to encompass elements scorned by many (mostly male) twentieth-century writers and critics. Warren explains, "Sentimentality requires an awareness of other people, a mental dialogue or displacement. The person who observes the sentiment-provoking situation must identify with or at least sympathize with the unfortunate person(s) whom he/she observes" (11). Joanne Dobson remarks, "Sentimentalism as construed by American women in the nineteenth century . . . is a complex imaginative phenomenon comprised . . . of feeling constellated around and valorizing a distinctive set of emotional priorities and a specific moral vision. . . . The sentimental imagination at its core manifests an irresistible impulse toward human connection" (170).[11] *The Storm* shares some characteristics with the tradition of the sentimental novel, particularly the importance of interpersonal relationships within a community. In fact, Jenny Greenough's isolation from her family in New York due to her removal to Key West and her husband's refusal to allow her to take part in the society that reaches out to her cause Jenny's misery. The toxic get-rich-quick world of the Key West man is unhealthy and unnatural.

Warren also mentions that "the implantation of virtue was the primary goal of nearly everything nineteenth-century Americans read: textbooks, novels, poems, magazine stories, or religious tracts" (157). *The Storm* does adhere to this pattern to some extent: Jenny at first follows a conventional path to virtue: she obeys her parents' wishes in marrying a man they approve of and she follows her husband's wishes to stay within her domestic sphere and not question his own behavior openly. Providence seems to reward her good behavior by sparing her from two disasters. However, *The Storm* deviates from the trend in novels that "used to be classed as 'literary sentimentality'" (Harris 265). Harris points out "that the large majority of nineteenth-century American women's novels have 'happy endings' in which their heroines marry and give up any idea of autonomy. . . . Despite following a fairly consistent pattern culminating in the protagonist's marriage to a dominating man, most sentimental novels also challenge the idea of female subordination, either through their plots, their narrators' addresses to the reader, or their patterns of rhetoric" (265). *The Storm* does have a happy ending, but the heroine actually escapes from a confining marriage by a turn of fortune in the plot: fate—or nature—removes the dominating man from her life, and her second marriage turns out to provide her with a good deal of autonomy and a fulfilling life.

The Storm at first resembles the domestic novels of the day, but the Key West tale challenges the domestic pattern significantly. According to Joyce Warren, domestic novel writers "celebrated domesticity, centering their fiction in woman and the home. . . . Reacting to their society's diminishment of women by investing the domestic role of women with supreme importance, they accepted their society's image of woman as passive, dependent, and domestic, but demonstrated that these very qualities gave women significance. . . . The first principle of the domestic novels is the necessity of selflessness and repression of the will" (7). Jenny Greenough tries to follow this principle and obey her husband's orders, but she becomes increasingly dissatisfied with her subordinate position. Warren argues, "Although [these writers] did not challenge the concept of male dominance, it is clear that they intended their definition of selflessness to apply to men as well as to women" (8). Part of *The Storm*'s success is in pointing out the hypocrisy of the separate spheres. Jenny—like Ellen Brown Anderson in her letters—does challenge male dominance in education and employment; she complains to herself about Peter's rules imposed on her, but she sees no way to change him and his completely selfish behavior. She escapes from her situation due to circumstances in which she has no agency, and the turn of events in the story implies that a man like Peter will never change: only a deus ex machina, in this case, the forces of nature, can rescue a women trapped in Jenny's position. Warren asserts, "It is no exaggeration to say that domestic fiction is preoccupied, even obsessed, with the nature of power. Because they lived in a society that celebrated free enterprise and democratic government but were excluded from participating in either, the two questions these female novelists never fail to ask are: what is power, and where is it located?" (160). For Jenny, power is control of one's own life; her education and society deprived her of options that would give her control of her life, and her first marriage confirmed her powerless situation. The true power lay in the parents who educated her for this life; in the patriarchal society that provided women an inferior education; and in her husband, who exploited the power dynamic sanctioned by that society. For Jenny, escape from oppression is a matter of chance, but she takes advantage of this chance to begin making her own choices and create a better life for herself.

Ellen Brown Anderson's challenging of the ideology surrounding the domestic sphere would award her a place within Warren's category of the questioners: "A significant group of women writers, whom we might call the questioners, criticized and questioned the assumptions of the dominant culture more than did the white male writers who were part of it. More explicit in some works than in others, this questioning took the form of negative character portrayal, thematic development, or explicit comment." All of these elements appear in *The Storm*.[12]

In many aspects, *The Storm* is a coming-of-age story displaying distinct characteristics of the bildungsroman, a novel of apprenticeship, education, or development. Appearing first in eighteenth-century Germany, this genre became increasingly popular during the nineteenth century. Jerome Buckley's *Season of Youth* (1974) discusses the genre's origin in Goethe's *Wilhelm Meister's Apprenticeship* (1794–1796) and identifies the following elements in it and similar novels:[13] "A child of some sensibility grows up ... [and] finds constraints, social and intellectual, placed upon [him].... His family ... proves antagonistic to his ambitions.... His first schooling ... may be frustrating insofar as it may suggest options not available to him in his present setting. He, therefore, sometimes at a quite early age, leaves the repressive atmosphere of home.... There his real education begins" (17).[14] *The Storm* follows this pattern in some ways, told from the perspective of Jenny Mansfield, a mature woman looking back on her earlier life as Jenny Greenough, married at age sixteen to twenty-nine-year-old Peter

Greenough. We find out little about her childhood, but her family's apparent antagonism to her forming any ambitions other than for marriage fits the bildungsroman pattern. For girls of Jenny's social class, coming of age meant being ready to marry, an age her parents thought she had reached. Jenny's education failed to prepare her for marriage—or for any other aspect of adult life.

As Elizabeth Abel, Marianne Hirsch, and Elizabeth Langland argue, "Clearly, successful *Bildung* requires the existence of a social context that will facilitate the unfolding of inner capacities, leading the young person from ignorance and innocence to wisdom and maturity. . . . Even the broadest definitions of the *Bildungsroman* presuppose a range of social options available only to men. . . . [Women] are not free to explore; more frequently, they merely exchange one domestic sphere for another" (6–8). This observation accurately describes Jenny's circumstances. Peter discourages her from taking part in Key West social life, and he disregards her other wishes. Even her appreciation of nature is restricted by the necessity of marital supervision: "[On the ship] I noticed . . . the bright trail of phosphorescent light, which heaves up round the bow and floats away in the wake of the vessel in warm climates, and I thought how magnificently and wonderfully this world was constructed, light and beauty breaking through darkness everywhere, and I wondered why young women could not be allowed to go about and admire it, without a protector, as our husbands call themselves" (19–20). Jenny Greenough clearly does not have the social options of the typical male protagonist of a bildungsroman and is given the chance to develop more fully only by chance.

Since Jenny Greenough cannot engage in the experiences necessary for the development of the protagonist, this story does not fit the original bildungsroman pattern. However, at about the time of *The Storm*'s composition, a "female version of the genre" developed; using examples such as Charlotte Brontë's *Jane Eyre* and George Eliot's *The Mill on the Floss*, the editors of *The Voyage In* explain that "in showing a continuous development from childhood to maturity, this paradigm adapts the linear structure of the male *Bildungsroman*" (11). E. H. Baruch argues that "unlike the male *bildungsroman*, the feminine *bildung* takes place in or on the periphery of marriage. That is its most striking characteristic" (335). She adds, "In [this] tradition . . . the heroine longs for a marriage that will increase her knowledge, often in some wide experiential sense" (336). Even after marriage, Jenny wants knowledge through travel, study, and social interaction, all of which Peter disregards. Peter in fact treats Jenny like a child. She overhears him tell Mrs. Cantwell, an attractive "woman of the world," (58) that she, Jenny, is "a mere doll" (40). *The Storm*'s illustrator clearly conveys Jenny's immaturity in two of the original pen-and-ink drawings (see figures 13 & 14).

When Jenny's attractive older sister, Melinda, and her husband move to the island, Jenny begins to feel even less like an adult: "Now occurred to me the meaning of being 'too young.' I could perceive that I was not a companion to my husband. I was simply a pet. . . . It was my sister who kept him from Mrs. Cantwell's. It was my sister who took him to task for gambling. . . . It was my sister who dared to rate him soundly if he did not attend properly to his business. . . . I felt somehow left out, and in the wrong place" (49–50). Jenny's awareness of her inadequacies as a married adult becomes the central concern of her life on the island.

Another way to see *The Storm* is as a "Novel of Awakening," a type of female bildungsroman that deviates more sharply from the male-centered framework than those mentioned above. Susan Rosowski identifies Flaubert's "*Madame Bovary* [as] a prototype for this pattern" (50). Emma Roualt, as an adolescent girl, often escaped from her dull, repressive life at school and home through "dreams of luxury and bliss" (50). She expects a happier life through marriage to Dr. Bovary, but "almost immediately, disparity between dream and reality is evident" (50). Similarly, Jenny's education prepared her to anticipate happiness in marriage, but, disappointed, she escapes into dreams. After Peter prevents her from accepting invitations to social events even when he is absent from home, she remarks, "I made no more attempts to go out, and the habit of solitary reverie I was forming was fast rendering all society insipid to me" (43). After Jenny hears longtime residents talk about their anticipation of an annual hurricane, this storm and her husband's imaginary heroism mingle within her daydreams: "This one terrible storm to come every year, seemed to be the superstition of the island, and it mingled largely in my imaginings. The hard work I prepared for poor Pete, and the desperate situations I contrived ways and means for him to get me out of, would be regarded as instances of the unreasonableness of women if I were to write them out; therefore, I say nothing more of my reveries" (43–44). Frustrated by her restricted life and her husband's neglect, she eagerly accepts her brother-in-law's offer to visit New York by steamboat. Once there, Jenny confides in her mother, who "warned me that nothing was worse for a young wife than to fall into discontent" (64).

Jenny reaches a state of near despair: "I began to believe not only that I had married too young, but that an age when I should arrive at sufficient wisdom for the state of matrimony would never be attained by me" (65). Jenny feels the full effect of her premature, compulsory coming of age. At a time when divorce was nearly impossible for women, she is bound to her unhappy marriage, one strictly divided by the established separate spheres—public for men and private for women. Jenny hurries back to Key West, and she resolves to win "the right place in [her] husband's affections" (66). Her ship approaches the island just as storm clouds appear in the distance.

Jenny soon learns that Peter and Melinda had departed that very morning to join her in New York. Jenny must face the hurricane, unhappy and alone, but Philip Mansfield, the lighthouse keeper's son, arrives and escorts her to "the Storm House, a place of safety built on the highest part of the island" (77). Jenny's story closely resembles the plot structure and character development usually found in the novel of awakening, a genre Susan Rosowski discusses in more detail: "The subject and action of the novel of awakening characteristically consist of a protagonist who attempts to find value in a world defined by love and marriage.... The protagonist's growth results typically not with 'an art of living' as for her male counterpart, but instead with a realization that for a woman such an art of living is difficult or impossible: it is an awakening to limitation" (49). For Jenny, her second coming of age, an awakening, begins with her discovery that her husband and sister had taken a ship bound not for New York but for England. They had betrayed her. The adulterous pair are found dead on the shore, their ship smashed by the storm. Jenny falls into delirium, but with the help of her friends, especially Philip, she recovers. The years before her marriage to Peter had failed to nurture Jenny into an adult, and her stifling marriage with Peter condemned her to a state of perpetual immaturity, but the storm rescues her from this fate. Jenny's unhappy Key West experiences have educated her, allowing her to develop adult awareness. However, rather than rush into the new life offered by a relationship with Philip Mansfield, Jenny demonstrates maturity by processing her experiences—reading, studying, and marrying Philip only when they can live together and travel as equal adults. Jenny truly comes of age this time. *The Storm,* ahead of its time in many respects, not only demonstrates the need for change in women's education and in the institution of marriage but also anticipates characteristics of female coming-of-age fiction that would gain popularity decades after its composition.

The Storm's Place in the Antebellum Literature of Florida and Key West

The Storm is distinctive in several ways: it is the first Florida hurricane story written by a woman, one of the first fictional treatments of the Florida Keys wrecking business, and probably the first novella written by any woman in Florida. This novella privileges not just Jenny's day-to-day existence but her unconventional challenges to her husband's drinking, her keen awareness of his infidelity, and her feeling of deserving a marriage rooted in mutual love and respect where she can serve as an equal partner. Most significantly, it is unique among Florida's antebellum fiction in presenting domestic life from a woman's point of view.[15]

Joyce Warren observes that, "for the most part, it was left to the nineteenth-century women writers to portray women as central. Moreover, not only were these works by women and about women, they portrayed life from the perspective of women" (1). Warren's claim fits *The Storm* nicely, but in addition to focusing on a woman's perspective, *The Storm* is the first Key West story with a female narrator. This narrator presents a woman's lonely domestic experience confined within the woman's sphere on this remote island and her psychological reaction to these conditions, quite a different experience from those of captivity narratives, shipwreck stories, or plantation tales.

Ellen Brown Anderson and Corinna Brown Aldrich never wrote for a Florida audience, which made sense for them due to the sparse population of most of the region during their years there and the absence of an established or cohesive literary community in Florida. Living in what was a frontier territory until 1845, far distant from booksellers and publishers, and sometimes even roughing it in log cabins, the sisters justifiably turned their attention to the cosmopolitan North where they had grown up. Most of their fictional writings therefore express little connection to Florida, except *The Storm* and one unfinished story, *Sketches of Life During the Second Seminole War*, whose only link to Florida is its title. Still, the title does suggest that if they had completed the story, the sisters would have incorporated into it some of the exciting personal experiences and anecdotes recorded in their letters written during the Second Seminole War.[16] It was Ellen, I believe, perhaps with some help from Corinna, who saw the potential of the Key West setting, with its energetic and diverse population, its dangerous waters, its community of daring rescue and salvage seamen, and its history of catastrophic weather.

As Maurice O'Sullivan makes clear, Florida has "the nation's oldest literary tradition" ("Interpreting Florida" 365), dating back to sixteenth-century Spanish and French exploration narratives, such as those of Peter Martyr d'Anghiera and Jean Ribaut.[17] In their surviving letters, Ellen and Corinna never mention previous or current Florida writers, and so they probably would not have realized that *The Storm* would become part of the rich literary tradition of Florida fiction that began with the novel *Atala*, written by French author François-René de Chateaubriand and published in 1801. *Atala*, narrated by a Natchez warrior, is partially set in Florida, but Chateaubriand himself probably never visited the territory.[18] According to Janette Gardner's bibliography, between 1801 and 1861, twenty-two works of fiction with a Florida setting were published.[19] The majority of these, like *Atala*, were written by authors who never lived in or even visited Florida. In contrast to this trend, Reverend Michael Smith's *The Lost Virgin of the South*, published in 1831, is, as O'Sullivan explains, "A fully Floridian novel, a book by a Florida resident, set largely in Florida and published in Tallahassee" (325). While *Atala* was the first novel to use Florida as a setting and to feature Native Americans on its soil, Smith's novel introduces two other seemingly inevitable plot elements that will appear later in *The Storm* and much other antebellum Florida fiction—storms and shipwrecks. *The Lost Virgin of the South* in fact opens with a storm and shipwreck in Biscayne Bay.[20] Eight years after Smith introduced the storm to Florida fiction, Robert Bird Montgomery, who most likely never visited Florida, added another storm to Florida literature with *The Adventures of Robin Day* (1839). In this picaresque novel,[21] Robin Day is captured by Creek warriors in Florida and taken to Alabama, but he escapes under the cover of a fierce storm. Also in 1839, the idea of escape during bad weather coincidentally appears in Henry William Herbert's *Ringwood the Rover: A Tale of Florida*. In this pirate story, Ringwood, the titular buccaneer, escapes from capture in St. Augustine under the cover of a hurricane. Writing under the pseudonym of Ned Buntline, Edward Zane Carroll Judson published *The Red Revenger: or, The Pirate King of Florida; A Romance of the Gulf and Its Islands*, in 1847.[22] In this pirate story, "the Red Revenger" is Rinard, who, in the book's opening, cruises the sea near Matacumba Key (now Matecumbe Key) as a gale approaches. The gale disables a nearby Spanish ship, but Rinard escapes with little damage and comes back for the storm's victims the next day. The following year, Judson, still writing as Ned Buntline, published *Matanzas: or, A Brother's Revenge; A Tale of Florida*—and again opens the story with a hurricane. Set in 1548, this novel begins with the Spanish territorial governor and his daughter watching from the battlements of the watch tower on Anastasia Island as the storm disables a French ship offshore. While *The Storm* also features a storm and a couple of shipwrecks, there is no evidence that the Brown sisters were influenced by any of these fictional works, but as highly active readers, they might well have read any of them.

A final consideration for *The Storm*'s place in Florida's literary history is the gender of its narrator and the apparent gender of its author. Since Ellen Anderson could not have written any of *The Storm* before 1849 and could not have finished it before 1853, the 1846 "Pirate of Key West," though it spends little more than a page on Key West and its treatment of Florida is secondhand, would make Hannah F. Gould the first woman to write or publish a work of fiction about Florida, and certainly about Key West. Another book, Madelaine H. Everett Donaldson's *The Thrilling Narrative and Extraordinary Adventures of Miss Madelaine H. Everett Who Was Abducted from the Bloomington Ladies' Seminary in Florida; and after Passing Through the Most Wonderful and Painful Scenes, Was Finally Rescued by Her Friends at an Auction Mart in Havana Where She Was About to Be Sold as a Slave*, published in 1849, occupies a more questionable place in the history of Florida literature. Although Gardner lists this as a work of fiction, the author presents it as an autobiographical captivity narrative. Since there is no biographical evidence of Madelaine Everett Donaldson ever having existed, the reader can assume that the author used a pseudonym, common enough in the nineteenth century for women writers, so who this author was or whether this writer had any direct experience of Florida remains unknowable. The facts that presumably form the foundation of the narrative itself first come into question in the book's title, which refers to "The Bloomington Ladies' Seminary in Florida," an institution that apparently never existed. The narrator explains that after being orphaned at a young age and passed around by shady adults, she ended up adopted by kind people who sent her to the Bloomington Ladies' Seminary in Bloomington, Florida, near Pensacola. Unfortunately, the town also never existed. To give the author the benefit of the doubt, the reader could assume this work to be entirely fictional and so accuracy of names and places would be irrelevant; or perhaps she was thinking of the Bloomington [Indiana] Female Academy, though that institution seems to have been more of a finishing school than a seminary and was quite far from Florida. She might also have been thinking of the Young Ladies Seminary and Collegiate Institute in Freeport, Florida. The only available information about this institution comes from an entry in ancestry.com displaying an image of the stately building that housed the school. Or perhaps the author was thinking about the Female Academy, which existed in Tallahassee from 1844 to 1858. In the story, the descriptions of the institution and its location are never specific, casting more doubt upon the author's knowledge of Florida.[23]

Caroline Lee Hentz, who moved to Marianna in 1852 and died there in 1856, is Florida's most significant antebellum woman writer, famous as "the South's leading fiction-writing apologist for the peculiar institution" (O'Sullivan 342). Hentz included Florida settings in two books, both published in 1852. *The Banished Son and Other Stories of the Heart* has two Florida selections. In "A Tale from the Land of Flowers," a young woman marries a soldier against her father's wishes, moves to his fort in Florida, and gets killed by a native warrior. "Magnolia Leaves" consists of rambling sketches written in Quincy, Florida. It includes descriptions of nature and ruins and comments on old letters, memories, and poems, but it says little about Florida. Partially set in the plantation belt of Middle Florida near the Georgia border, *Marcus Warland: Or, The Long Moss Spring: A Tale of the South*, a novel, presents a fantasy world at the fictional Bellamy Plantation, where enslaved people and their captors love one another in a harmonious relationship.[24]

One of the most intriguing works of antebellum Florida fiction was apparently written in 1855, about the time of *The Storm*'s composition, and, like it, remained unpublished until very recently. The manuscript for Cyrus Parkhurst Condit's *A Trip to Florida for Health and Sport* was recently discovered, edited, and published by Maurice O'Sullivan and Wenxian Zhang, professors at Rollins College.[25] The editors believe that the manuscript was a first draft and that "the story's incidents are so circumstantial in detail that they appear clearly based on first-hand experience or taken from familiar local anecdote" (ix). The novel is a fictional account of the experiences of young George Morton, who becomes sickly after his father dies and whose mother sends him with his Uncle James to Florida to recover his strength through exercise in the warm climate. Many significant qualities of *A Trip to Florida* resemble aspects of *The Storm*. For instance, as the editors observe, "In describing how the handful of Welaka residents and the farmers who surrounded them worked and socialized, married and worshipped, hunted and fished, Condit has made a rich contribution to our understanding of antebellum Florida" (ix). Much the same can be said for *The Storm* in its depiction of the community life of Key West.

O'Sullivan and Zhang comment that "by the mid-1850's only ten novels had been set in the state [and] . . . most of those novelists look either to the past or to the complex diversity of the region's population for tales that mix adventure and romance, legend and history" (ix). They add that, "unlike those books, or the handful of other early Florida novels, *A Trip to Florida for Health and Sport* is a quietly domestic account of everyday life in the new state of Florida" (X). Similarly, *The Storm* takes place in antebellum Key West and provides details about the everyday domestic, social, and business life of the island community; the depiction of domestic life from a woman's viewpoint appears nowhere else in Florida's antebellum fiction. Perhaps the most interesting similarity between the two works is that both are coming-of-age stories with young protagonists from the North who gain experience and maturity during their time in Florida, after which each returns home. *A Trip to Florida*'s George Morton, age seventeen, and Jenny Greenough, age sixteen, both grew up in New York City; significantly, however, George has been well educated, first at a country boarding school and then in the city before he becomes sick and is sent to Florida. Jenny's gender-limited education is a major source of bitterness for her, as is the lack of freedom to enjoy the kind of experiences that George has. George's story takes place mostly outdoors and includes many traditionally male activities such as hunting, fishing, exploring, and meeting interesting characters, while Jenny's story focuses on her circumscribed domestic role as a young married woman. Jenny's married status makes her coming-of-age story unusual, but her experiences in Key West allow her to start over as a more mature young woman, ready to deal with life as a responsible adult in a second, much healthier marriage.[26]

The absentee authorship of most antebellum nineteenth-century fiction about Florida is especially pronounced in Keys fiction: of the four published antebellum works of fiction that use Key West or nearby waters to some degree for their settings, none of the authors seems to have traveled to Key West, the other keys, or even Florida. As Maureen Ogle remarks concerning nineteenth-century writing about Key West, "Fiction writers who never came anywhere near the place contributed to the island's growing mythology, weaving Keys tales of pirate desperadoes who skulked about digging for treasure and preying on the innocent" (38). Despite Key West's geographical isolation from the rest of Florida and the United States, these authors had many sources of information about the bustling island, the most heavily populated city in Florida by 1850. The U.S. Navy base and the regular steamboat line running from Key West to New York meant that these authors could have known sailors or travelers with firsthand accounts of the island, and multiple periodicals, such as the *New York Herald*, the *New Orleans Daily Picayune*, and the *Baltimore Sun*, published articles about Key West. Other publications, such as John James Audubon's *Ornithological Biography* . . . (1832), which includes an appearance by wreckers, were readily available. The first of these Keys stories, "The Florida Pirate," published in Edinburgh, Scotland, in 1821 by Scottish travel and fiction writer John Howison, takes place in the Straits of Florida directly south of Key West, but the action never carries over to the island itself. Regardless of its promising title, Joseph Holt Ingraham's *Rafael, or, The Twice Condemned: A Tale of Key West* (1845) has little to do with the island. Set in 1840, this book opens on board a U.S. military ship, *The Dolphin*, which rushes from the Key West port to rescue a merchant brig from a pursuing pirate; after this, Key West plays no significant role.

The Storm is not the first work of fiction to mention the Key West shipwreck-salvaging business and the "wreckers" who manned the salvage boats, but it offers the only extended antebellum literary account of this intriguing profession. In "The Pirate of Key West," published in *Godey's Lady's Book* in 1846 by H. F. Gould, the author begins by describing Key West, then briefly mentions wreckers and defends their integrity;[27] however, after about a page, she begins spinning a sentimental tale about a reformed pirate who goes home to his small Massachusetts town to live out his old age piously. James Fenimore Cooper's *Jack Tier: or, The Florida Reef* (1848) also mentions wreckers. According to biographer Franklin Wayne, Cooper never actually sailed farther south than Chesapeake Bay, but his nautical knowledge was solid since he spent several years as a sailor on merchant ships and two as a midshipman in the U.S. Navy. His depiction of the Keys reflects his reading and various conversations with friends and relatives who had been there (Wayne 391–92). Whenever the tale's narrator mentions wreckers, he offers no specific details, but when one of the novel's main characters, Captain Spike—himself a treacherous smuggler—comments on the dangers of the reef, he refers to "them devils of wreckers" and complains, "Let this brig only get fast upon a rock, and they would turn up, like sharks, all around us, each with his maw open for salvage" (Cooper 271). Later, when the brig and a schooner are wrecked on the reef, the wreckers manage to raise the schooner and salvage what they can from the ruined brig. In chapter 5, Cooper's extensive experience as a sailor shows in his meticulous account of the crew of the brig *The Molly*

Swash raising a Mexican schooner sunk by a tornado. Although *The Molly Swash* is not a wrecker, the scene demonstrates in fascinating detail how one ship can raise another and restore it to sailing condition. Nevertheless, for antebellum fiction that treats Key West and its wrecking business with any detail—apparently drawn from firsthand observation—the reader must turn to *The Storm*.

Given the probability of its having been completed sometime between 1854 and 1862, *The Storm* cannot lay claim to being the first work of fiction written by a woman using a Florida, or even a Key West, setting. Still, placed in the context of other antebellum Florida literature, *The Storm* appears distinctive in several ways: it is probably the first Key West story written by a woman with personal experience of Key West, the first Key West story with a female narrator and protagonist, the first Florida hurricane story written by a woman, one of the first fictional treatments of the Florida Keys wrecking business, and probably the first novella written by any woman in Florida.

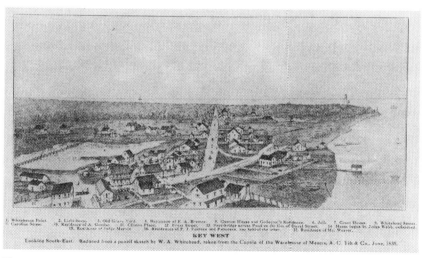

Figure 5. Pencil sketch of Key West, Florida, by W. A. Whitehead, taken from the cupola of the warehouse of Messrs. A. C. Tift & Co., June 1838. This image is of special interest since the lighthouse that was destroyed in the 1846 hurricane and the old cemetery that was flooded are pinpointed in this drawing—and are featured in *The Storm*. Photograph credit: "Naval History 7 Heritage Command Photo Section, Photo #NH 122419."

Notes

1 James M. Denham and I conducted extensive research on the Brown sisters and published an edited selection of their letters, *Echoes from a Distant Frontier*. We have also cowritten another book and several articles on the family and their letters, and I have written several articles on the sisters' literary efforts. See the works cited and consulted list for full references.

2 For more information about Corinna and Ellen's family, see Denham and Huneycutt, *Echoes from a Distant Frontier*, xviii–xxii.

3 Had the Brown sisters completed this story, it could have contributed to the body of fiction about the Seminoles and other Native American tribes in Florida. O'Sullivan explains in "Interpreting Florida" that "the displacement of Native Americans from their territory remained at the core of Florida's early fiction" (328). Gardner's *Annotated Bibliography of Florida Fiction, 1801–1980*, lists eleven works of antebellum fiction that include Seminoles or members of other Florida tribes.

4 Augusta Jane Evans's *Beulah: a Novel*, was first published in 1859.

5 See *Echoes from a Distant Frontier*, 282–85, for more information about Corinna's debilitating condition.

6 For information about this powerful hurricane, see Corey Malcolm, "Understanding the Key West Hurricane of 1846"; Jay Barnes, *Florida's Hurricane History*, 59–60; Walter Maloney, *A Sketch of the History of Key West, Florida*, 41; Maureen Ogle, *Key West: History of an Island of Dreams*, 41–42; and Canter Brown, *Ossian Bingley Hart*, 68–74.

7 According to Dorothy Dodd, in 1851, twenty-seven shipwreck salvaging vessels, or wreckers, operated on the Florida Reef and carried salvaged goods to Key West (186). For an in-depth discussion of shipwreck salvage operations based on contemporary sources, see Dodd's "The Wrecking Business on the Florida Reef." See also Scott and Walker's "The City of Wreckers: Two Key West Letters of 1838." Maureen Ogle points out in *Key West* that "the nation's commercial press and the insurance industry castigated Key West wreckers as nothing more than licensed pirates who profited from others' woes and conspired with lighthouse keepers to cause wrecks." She adds, "In reality, and despite the occasional murder or duel (neither of which was unusual in early-nineteenth-century America), life on Key West never came close to the reputation concocted by novelists, journalists, and rumor" (38). See also the short PBS documentary, "Key West Wreckers," at https://www.pbs.org/video/wlrn-history-key-west-wreckers/.

8 For more on Captain Brown and his privateering career, see *Echoes from a Distant Frontier*, xix–xx.

9 Ideas informing the argument of Wollstonecraft's seminal feminist text—and also the first wave of American feminism—seem to reverberate throughout the story. For instance, Jenny Greenough feels totally unprepared for any occupation or pursuit other than that of being a wife, similar to Wollstonecraft's complaint that the English educational system leaves women unprepared for occupations besides those of wife and mother. Jenny feels inadequate in her role as a wife because she believes

that her lack of education has left her uninteresting to her husband. Wollstonecraft's argument that educated women would be more virtuous and could serve to better regulate their husbands' morality seems borne out by Jenny's inability to improve her husband.

10 Wells remarks in *Women Writers and Journalists in the Nineteenth-Century South* that "postal records demonstrate clearly that men and women in the South subscribed in surprisingly large numbers to periodicals from the North" (62). He adds, "The number of titles, as well as the sophistication and diversity of magazines, increased dramatically after about 1820 nationwide. One chief reason for their expansion was the improvement of the postal delivery system. . . . Every major southern town and city had at least one periodical, and often several could be purchased through subscriptions or through local bookstores" (65).

11 Speaking of popular sentimental fiction such as Susan Warner's *The Wide, Wide World* (1850), *Uncle Tom's Cabin* (1852), and Maria Cummins's *The Lamplighter* (1854), Jane Tompkins argues in *Sensational Designs* that the popularity of such fiction reflects the mainstream culture in which it was published (148–49): "Such stories filled the religious publications distributed in unimaginably large quantities by organizations like those of the Evangelical United Front. . . . . And the same kind of exemplary narrative was the staple of the McGuffey's readers and primers of a similar type on which virtually the entire nation had been schooled. They appeared in manuals of social behavior, and in instructional literature of every variety, filled the pages of popular magazines, and appeared even in the daily newspapers. As David Reynolds has recently demonstrated, the entire practice of pulpit oratory in this period shifted from an expository and abstract mode of explicating religious doctrine, to a mode in which sensational narratives carried the burden of theological precept" (153).

12 See appendix B of this book for a brief analysis of *The Storm* in the context of nineteenth-century women's social status and marriage.

13 James N. Hardin explains in *Reflection and Action* that "the word *Bildungsroman* was coined in 1819 by an obscure professor of rhetoric in Dorpat, Karl von Morgenstern, [who] linked the word *Bildung* to the hero's development and experience, to his education, and to the *Bildung* [culture] of the reader" (xiii–xiv).

14 For another excellent history of the origin of the genre, its development and variations, and a survey of critical discussions of the American and British traditions, see the introduction to Kelsey L. Bennett's *Principle and Propensity*.

15 Considering *The Storm* within antebellum literature is appropriate since topical references place the setting in the mid-nineteenth century and the story does not refer to the Civil War. Also, Ellen Brown Anderson, the apparent primary author of this story, died in 1862, a little more than a year after hostilities erupted; during that final year, she was too sick for much writing and focused most of her energy on making arrangements for her daughters' care after her death. If the final few pages of *The Storm* seem hurried compared to the rest of the story, perhaps it is because Ellen felt a sense of urgency to complete it as her health declined. She was keenly aware that her death approached.

16 See appendix B for a brief discussion of this story fragment.
17 For samples of early Florida writings, with helpful commentary by the editors, see Maurice O'Sullivan and Jack C. Lane's *The Florida Reader*.
18 For a discussion of this novel's interpretation of Florida as a natural paradise and of the novel's impact on American and world literature, see O'Sullivan's "Interpreting Florida," 322–25. Also see O'Sullivan and Zhang's discussion in their edition of Conduit's *A Trip to Florida for Health and Sport*, 131–33.
19 The bibliography actually lists twenty-three, but one of them, Mrs. Mary Andrews Denison's *Florida, or, The Iron Will: A Story of Today* (1861), is set in Connecticut. Florida is the name of a character in this dime novel. However, including *A Trip to Florida for Health and Sport*, as yet undiscovered when Gardner published her book, the number comes back to twenty-three. It is best to consider the number as approximate.
20 For a summary and analysis of this "remarkably confusing narrative" (O'Sullivan 326), see O'Sullivan, "Interpreting Florida," 325–28.
21 See O'Sullivan, "Interpreting Florida," 331.
22 Judson did have firsthand knowledge of Florida. O'Sullivan notes in "Interpreting Florida" that Judson "served in the U.S. Navy's Mosquito Fleet during the Second Seminole War" (334).
23 For more about the Bloomington Female Academy, see Bill Kemp's "Major's Female College Was an Early Bloomington School for Young Women." For more about the Female Academy in Tallahassee, see William G. Dodd's "Early Education in Tallahassee and the West Florida Seminary, Now Florida State University."
24 For discussions of this novel, see O'Sullivan, "Interpreting Florida," 342–43, and Carole Policy's "Defending the Middle Florida Plantation," 81–89.
25 For information about the manuscript's discovery and the editing process and also for historical background and literary context, see O'Sullivan and Zhang, eds., *A Trip to Florida for Health and Sport*, ix–xx and 129–46.
26 For an analysis of George's maturing process, see O'Sullivan and Zhang, eds., *A Trip to Florida for Health and Sport*, 138–42.
27 A possible source for Gould's favorable comments concerning wreckers is Audubon's "The Wreckers of Florida" in *Ornithological Biography*, 3:158–63. Audubon's account of his encounter with the wreckers challenged the once-widely held prejudices against them. After getting to know "these excellent fellows," he remarked, "how different, thought I, is often the knowledge of things acquired by personal observation, from that obtained by report!" (160).

Figure 6. Key West, 1849. According to the Florida Memory website, "This daguerreotype is one of the oldest photographs ever taken in Florida. It dates to about 1849 and was likely taken from an observation tower or rooftop on the northwest side of Key West near the corner of Front and Whitehead streets. Like most daguerreotypes, the image is reversed. Visible near the horizon are St. Paul's Episcopal Church (left) and First Baptist Church (middle), both located on Eaton Street." Longtime Episcopalians, Corinna and Ellen would most likely have attended St. Paul's while they were in Key West. Many of these structures were either new or recently rebuilt since most of the island's buildings had been destroyed by the hurricane of 1846. *Bird's eye view overlooking various buildings in downtown Key West.* 1849 (circa). State Archives of Florida, Florida Memory. Accessed October 22, 2023. https://www.floridamemory.com/items/show/4962

Figure 7. Engraving of wreckers at work. Photonegative of an engraving published in *Harper's New Monthly Magazine* 18, page 577, 1858/1859. Florida Memory, Florida State Archives. Public Domain.

Figure 8. Photograph of Corinna Georgia Anderson, 1865 or later. Ellen's oldest daughter and amanuensis, Georgia was most likely the copyist of the manuscript of *The Storm*. Courtesy of Jane and Raymond Gill and Elizabeth Traynor.

Figure 9. Ellen Mannevillette ("Villette") Anderson, 1865 or later. Ellen's youngest child, Villette was a professional illustrator who might have made or assisted with the three drawings accompanying the manuscript of *The Storm*. Courtesy of Jane and Raymond Gill and Elizabeth Traynor.

Figure 10. Photograph of Ellen Brown Anderson, circa 1855. Courtesy of Jane and Raymond Gill and Elizabeth Traynor.

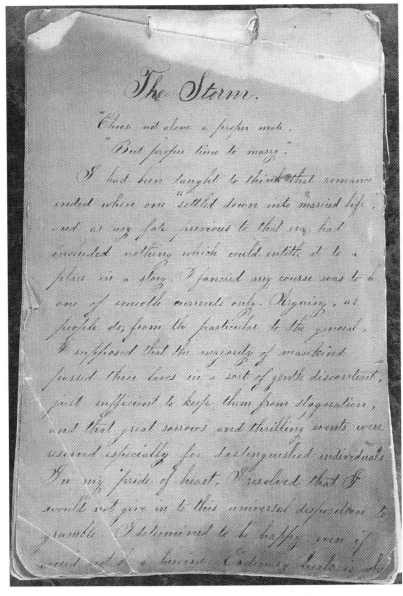

Figure 11. Photograph of the title page of *The Storm*. The manuscript, which was completed between 1853 and 1862, is now stored in the special collections of the P. K. Yonge Library of Florida History at the University of Florida, Gainesville. The paper, otherwise generally in good condition, is faded around the edges of some pages from exposure to light, especially the title page, but the writing is generally clear throughout the ninety-page manuscript. Courtesy of Jane and Raymond Gill and Elizabeth Traynor.

The Storm

*"Choose not alone a proper mate,
But proper time to marry."*[1]

I had been taught to think that romance ended when one "settled down into married life," and as my fate previous to that era had included nothing which could entitle it to a place in a story, I fancied my course was to be one of smooth currents only. Arguing, as people do, from the particular to the general, I supposed that the majority of mankind passed their lives in a sort of gentle discontent, just sufficient to keep them from stagnation, and that great sorrows and their thrilling events were reserved specifically for distinguished individuals.

In my pride of heart, I resolved that I would not give in to this universal disposition to grumble. I determined to be happy, even if I would not be a heroine. Ordinary luck is what

[2][2]

an ordinary mortal has a right to expect, and they are unwise and conceited who look for more. Our Heavenly Father has meted out happiness to us in equal quantities, but like the workmen paid at the end of the day, each complains because he receives no more than his neighbor, and all put in a plea that they have borne the burden and heat of the day. He that has, is like enough to find himself distinguished, but if ambition expects more for its wages than the penny's worth of happiness at the close of the day, its success will prove a disappointment — as it is, almost always. But I had no talents on which to base an ambition. I should designate myself a negative woman, being neither tall nor short, handsome nor ugly, wise nor silly, but in fact altogether of the medium sort, and yet I determined to be content with my lot.

Would any one like to learn a lesson from me? I am an indifferent writer, but I will

[3]

tell my story, although like other uncultivated fruit, it may merely remind of that which might be good.

I was married at the early age of sixteen. "Too young," said the grumblers. But why too young, I asked. No objection was made to the gentleman who stood to me in the position of husband and protector. He was twenty nine, a physician with fair prospects. It was pronounced an act of duty and of preeminent good sense, on *his* part, to marry. Nor do I remember that any one said distinctly that I was too young for him. I am of opinion that whoever had disputed his ability to judge for himself in such matters, would have received a tart answer.

So it happened that I was married in the most commonplace way. My mother fussed herself prodigiously with cake, company and dresses. Blessings on her, she surely carried my burdens, so long as I was a child. I never doubted that I should be dressed to perfection, that the

[4]

cake, the company, and the arrangements altogether, would proceed with a rightness, which no other super-intendence could improve. My father took me upon his knee more often, and caressed me more fondly, than had been his wont, but no objection was made to my marriage. They, in conjunction with the rest of the world, believed that a young woman was born, destined, fore-ordained and com-missioned to get married. The time and manner of that event might be matter for consideration, but upon the whole, like murder in the estimation of Lady Macbeth; "If it were well done, when it were done, then it were well it were done quickly." My mother had a pretty way of complaining that she could not keep her daughters on hand, and my father used to wish the young fellows away without a frown, and invite them to the house most smilingly.

[5]

At the time of my marriage, I had a sister, also married, who was travelling in Europe with her husband, and it was one of my small regrets, that in consequence of marrying a physician, whose profession, it was said, ought to confine him to one spot of Earth, I should probably never enjoy that heaven of American glory, — a visit to Paris.

As I was in the habit of saying everything I thought, Pete — my husband's name was Peter, but then he had lovely eyes, I would have shortened it into Pet, but I was afraid of being thought silly. However, as I was saying,

Pete fished up this small discontent from my clear stream of happiness, and removed it, by telling me that as soon as he was able, — and he intended to be rich in an incredibly short space of time — it was part of his plan of life to go to Europe, and there pursue his profession with a view to seeing and learning, all which could be ascertained on the subject of the human form divine.

[6]

Ah, poor Pete! did not I sixteen years old and bothered to put up my hair, which was in that uncomfortable condition known to young ladies as neither short nor long — didn't I think him a great man! Did I not determine to be a help meet for him! With what zeal I looked forward to my new duties of housekeeper and wife of a poor man, as I considered him! As if any man were poor with abounding health, prosperous business, and a devoted wife. We shall see. There was a serpent in Eden, and those who look for a paradise without some such ugly customer, must seek it in worlds beyond our mortal ken.

Away, beyond that southernmost portion of our land which reaches almost down to the tropic of Cancer, and seems to point meddlesomely towards the West Indies, there is an island, where reigns a perpetual and delicious summer. There, the nearly vertical sun is ever tempered by the cool sea breeze; and there the frost of winter never casts its blight.

[7]

Although not within the Torrid, the trees and shrubs there quit all characteristics of the Temperate zone; and one might fancy in that isolated mixture of the two climates, that he breathed the air of paradise, were it not that amid the delights of earth and sky, there swarm the mosquitoes like the flies of Egypt,[3] and there dwell men, with their passions, their cares, and their thirst of gain.

This island of Key West, then almost unknown, was chosen by my husband as the locality most favorable to the cultivation of a fortune. Many years ago the spot was looked upon as a mere nest of Pirates, — a word at that time almost synonymous with wreckers. My husband was a man capable of perceiving the true character of the vocation then held in bad repute. He has been wrecked among those deceitfully calm waters, and rescued by these brave fellows who spent their lives in perils and adventures of the wildest sort, and laughed at, rather gloried

[8]

in their bad reputation. All the little settlements in that region of difficult and dangerous navigation, are composed of wreckers, or persons who draw their support from that business, and a curious one it is, requiring skill, courage, and patience in no ordinary degree. By it, a man will sometimes win a fair fortune in a short time; again no wrecks during a lazy spell will plunge him back into poverty, for his vessel must be ever in repair, and his men ready at a moment's warning. Generally, the wrecking vessels are owned in partnership, and measured by a sort of stock company, as are whale ships. The owners supply the sailors with food, and they occupy various stations, among the reefs, whence, in sunshine and in storms, they cruise about in the vicinity, or lay to and watch, ever ready to help and to save the unfortunate mariner.

[9]

A moment's reflection would teach us, that outside of large cities which like great nets cast into the sea, gather fish of every kind—small communities collect such characters as are called for by the natural surroundings of the locality. Thus, as a general thing we do not find old sailors settling down on backwoods farms, nor the outpourings of colleges, collected amid the storms of old ocean. When we meet with individuals thus apparently out of place, we know them to be exceptions to the general rule, and we look for some idiosyncrasy, in consonance with their excentric[4] position. One of these exceptional cases was my husband. Raised in a small New England seaport, he was destined a physician from the mere fact that his father had been one before him. In consequence of that, it was the handiest profession for him to choose, and he was not possessed of force of will, which seizes the reigns of destiny, and turns from his path the bounding steed of circumstance.

[10]

With a vivid imagination, enthusiastic temperament, and physically brave, he wearied of the tame charms of a Yankee village. Speedy wealth and daring adventure, were the sirens who sung to him among the sandbanks of the gulf, and lured him to their Scylla and Charybdis of freedom from restraint.

I have said before that he had been shipwrecked, but it was not in a storm. It is not generally known that calms in that locality are as dangerous as storms. The drifting sea seems so glassy and still, a landsman is surprised at the captain's troubled countenance, and finds it hard to believe that, like a deceitful friend, the current is fast carrying him among shoals and coral reefs. Vainly the watchman sees the breakers. Without the friendly wind, there is no earthly power to arrest the vessel's course. The wildest storm is perhaps less trying to the nerves of a strong, able sailor, than those most powerful, most placid, but utterly resistless calms, which allow the ever

[11]

changing currents to fix his vessel hard and fast upon the coral reefs, while the sails flap idly against the mast, the sun shines out clear in the heavens, and the ocean is smooth as a mirror.

At such times the sailors, sitting about the vessel, singing and mending their sails, and telling their strange stories of sea life, remind one that extremes meet. They, as a class the bravest of the brave, and the hardiest of the hardy, have in their leisure moments the habits of ladies: they sew.

My husband had been a passenger in a vessel thus becalmed, had been upon the reefs and been rescued from his perilous situation. Perilous though calm! Ah, life is full of such dangerous navigation.

Think of the terrors of such a condition. In mid ocean, with no beach, no landing place in sight, fast jammed upon the coral reef, and the all-powerful current still forcing them

[12]

farther on, while no change of weather can loose them from its grasp, except that the storm, ever murmuring in the distance, should sweep it with wild waves, and dash them to a more speedy, although not less certain, destruction. Oh, then how welcome the light and graceful wreckers! —so perfectly modeled, so splendidly kept, that almost they sail without a wind, — with captains who are indeed familiar with old ocean, for they have sounded its very depth, marked its every current, and noted its daily change. No dangers appal and no hardships deter them. In the sickening calm, and the roaring storm; on the dangerous shoals and amid the eddying breakers; they come with their strong arms, and thorough knowledge, to relieve and to rescue; and so well do they understand their business, and so prepared are they for every emergency, that now, it is said, never (except in those terrible tempests in which no vessel can live) is a human life lost, amid all the wrecks which yearly strew that dangerous coast.

[13]

The little vessels float over those dangerous waters like white-winged angels of mercy, and make us indignant that such should have been associated with the hateful name of pirate. Whatever the wreckers might have been in the beginning, my husband found them generous, open hearted and merciful, saving life always in preference to property, with such failings otherwise as are shared by mankind in general. When he returned from that southern trip, which was shortly before our marriage—it was easy to tell that he had been among congenial beings. He had seen a prospect of more surgery than physic, and he determined to cast his lot among them.

To which intention I made no objection, for my hopes had caught their coloring from his, and it was with the most earnest sympathy in all his undertakings, that I embarked with him from my Northern home, to go to my strange residence in the far South. Thus the first great impulse of my destiny received its direction from a deceitful calm.

[14]

It was the first time I had ever been at sea, and fortunately I was not sick. Oh, how I enjoyed it! Everything was new to me. There was a strong fair wind blowing, the Captain was cheerful, the sailors busy, and our little craft shot over the water like a sea-gull. She bounded up and down upon the waves, and occasionally shipped a sea which foamed over the bow and passed along out at the side giving me the idea—I am afraid very childish—that the vessel was too light, and trifling, a thing to sink. She seemed a sea pony endowed with wings, what my dear father would have denominated "as easy going critter, quite free and sprightly."

Never shall I forget the moonlights and starlights, the sunrisings and sunsettings of that to me most novel voyage. With the streets, and the houses, and the lands removed, with what wonderful new developments, comes up the scenery of the heavens. Sometimes hanging low and dark, the clouds seem to crowd down upon us, and we glide, as it were through

[15]

walls of water, by a pale ghostly light; then they break and float away, piling themselves in dark mountains against the horizon, while the sun pours floods of glorious light on sea, and sky, and cloud. The vastness of the firmament, which, in the clear atmosphere of the gulf, seems larger than elsewhere, and vividness of the stars, and the murmuring rush, when the wind opposes the current, are things peculiar to that far Southern latitude; the recollection of them lingers in my memory as a gallery of pictures, painted by no mortal hand. I have sat amid sparkling sunlight, and seen in the distance, three tiers of clouds hanging high, oh, so high! Those trees of the ocean—one over another, and pouring their stormy rush of rain, from cloud to cloud below, down, down, the last and most violent upon — what? Perhaps a distant ship. I was safe, and far from danger. The same high power which shielded me, governed that distant storm. Oh, how happy I was, while the white winged vessel was bearing me away past rocks, past breakers, to

[16]

that distant shore where the storm of my life was to culminate.

"I am sorry to break my pace so suddenly," is an apology an amiable horse might be supposed to make to his rider, when striking a sharp stone, has caused him to limp, instead of amble, and I feel inclined to say something of the kind, as I feel the sharp sting of memory when I recall my first annoyance on drawing near the harbor of my home and hopes. Every person is said to have a besetting sin. By parity of reasoning, every place should have it also. The besetting sin of Key West is mosquitoes. Oh, the mosquitoes! The blood thirsty, persecuting, persevering mosquitoes! Does anyone think them a trifle? That person has not been to Key West. Does any man dare to pho-pho them? The writer of this history has known an army to be turned back by them, and military operations delayed for defenses against them, in Florida, —

[17]

and not without reason. What were mosquitoes made for? The purpose for which they were introduced into this otherwise inhabitable world is to my tortured understanding, an inexplicable mystery and will forever remain so. I could not help grumbling a little, when I found myself forced to choose between being flayed alive, or smothered in dagger-proof clothing.

I know you are dying of curiosity to know why I have never mentioned my husband, all this time. In truth he was beginning to lose many of his fine qualities in my estimation. He was so sure of me, after we were married, that he grew quite pert and impertinent.

Your handsome man is such a ladies' pet, that it is running a great risk for an ordinary woman to marry one; and Pete was a handsome fellow with fine eyes, curling hair and a dashing manner, but then he would get cross, and swear out of those fine mustaches of his, and would go down in the cabin, and play cards by the hour, and drink molasses and water as he called it,

[18]

although I knew he hated molasses, and would neither eat nor drink it, in my mother's house. I suspected him of playing the hypocrite a little in this matter, so I said to him, one evening, when he came up and sat down beside me, as I was looking over the side of the vessel, 'Pete, molasses has, as poor mother used to say, a very rummy smell, in this latitude." Whereupon he became very angry, and wished to know if I had anything to say, why I did not speak out, and not insinuate in that mean way. I thought I had spoken out, but he walked off, and I remained looking over the side of the vessel. Then I noticed, for the first time, the bright trail of phosphorescent light, which heaves up round the bow, and floats away in the wake, of the vessel in warm climates, and I thought how magnificently and wonderfully, this world was constructed,

[19]

light and beauty breaking through darkness everywhere, and I wondered why young women could not be allowed to go about and admire it, without a protector, as our husbands call themselves.

After that night, I did not say anything more to Pete about drinking, because I did not like to have him cross. I have often wondered how he came to like me. I think it must have been because I was so indifferent to him. I have often observed that men, who are generally admired by women, always give their particular preferences to those who take little notice of them. This must be mere curiosity, and love of conquest. I saw that Pete, like Judah, was a lion among men, and for that very reason, never supposed he could fall to my humble lot, but when he convinced me as, right or wrong, convince me he did, that I, an insignificant school girl, held his happiness in my tiny power, the magnitude of the responsibility, seemed to change my nature.[5] I did love him. All in my nature which could be called affection, was concentrated and bestowed upon

[20]

him. But when this became my state of feeling, I seemed to lose my value. Perhaps it was my too great anxiety to please. At any rate I grew thoughtful, and Pete said I moped. I did not blame him. I felt stupid, and so I was willing he should go where he could be better entertained.

We arrived in the morning, but I remember nothing rational, nothing in fact but mosquitoes, from the time we neared the land, until I found myself upon the premises of my new home. Here were still the mosquitoes—the inevitable, irrepressible, unconquerable mosquitoes, but the place was so enchantingly beautiful, that, even amid these inquisitors, I was forced to admire.

The cool sea breeze came sweeping in from the ocean, swaying and waving the plantain and banana, and lifting and bending the long leaves of the cocoa nut in their plume-like motion. In view of the sea, on a slight rise of ground stood my bijou of a house, sheltered beneath a

[21] cluster of tropical trees and embedded in shrubbery and flowers. It was a very sailor's dream, built of wood, of course, but painted to resemble marble, and by making believe just enough to suppose it marble, its beauty was greatly enhanced. Nevertheless, it was a sweet, pretty design, and well executed, although the material of which it was made, had been hewn out of logs, instead of having been dug out of quarries. A row of white columns with Doric capitals, supported the roof of a piazza, which extended entirely around the building. Upon the eaves of this, was a light balustrade, that formed a balcony in front of the second story, extending only one third of the building, and a parapet around the one story wings. These wings were canopied over with the long, branch-like leaves of the cocoanut trees. The rose and the lime tree, the hybiscus [sic], the cactus, and the geranium, scented the air of the surrounding garden, or

[22] gemmed it with their brilliant flowers, while the almond tree, the oleander, and the ligistranium[6] mingled with the palm and the cocoa-nut, to shade it. Around the pillars of the piazza wound the beautiful salina with its bright blue flowers.[7] The ascent to the roof, was by stairs outside the house, so that we could run all over our dwelling, like the ants and bees, without going into it. When I tell you what we could see from it, you will think that no small privilege.

The house within, upon the ground floor, was composed of three rooms, opening in to each other with folding doors, high and wide, so that the three rooms could be thrown into one at pleasure. The means of egress were either windows or doors, at the option of the speaker, for they were all alike composed of glass, and closed only when the wind took an inconvenient direction, or when it was *cool*. It is never *cold* in Key West. At the time of which I write, there

[23] were no places for fire in the dwelling houses. The kitchen in all Florida is always a separate building. A globe lamp and closed doors, was sufficient warming apparatus in Key West for a parlor. They affect chimneys[8] now, and entertain a newspaper, but I am an antediluvian.

All this time, I was industriously slaying the mosquitoes, and when weary of wielding my fan, I would only vary the exercise by slapping my own face. But oh, the comfort, the peace, the surprise, which awaited me in the parlor! In the centre of the room was a large tent of fine white lace, fastened to a large ring near the ceiling; it fell upon the floor terminated by a heavy fringe, which gave weight to the lace, lest too light a breath of air should carelessly lift a fold, and let in the watchful enemy. I sprang into this haven of rest, sat down upon a tete-a-tete there, and drew a long breath of relief. While I fancy myself sitting there in coolness and comfort, I will tell you

[24]

a little about my furniture.

There were no carpets upon the floor — the very idea of them in that climate is uncomfortable — but straw-matting instead. The rooms were not crowded, but whatever was there was excellent of its kind, and the whole comprised a sort of miniature world's fair. Remember that this was the home of the wreckers, and our houses were furnished with the treasures of the deep. There was a fine large mirror of English workmanship, a set of French chairs, a bust of Josephine, and a picture representing the same lady. There was a fine case of books containing about a hundred volumes, and on the top of it a clock, which especially pleased my taste. Four Corinthian pillars of alabaster supported the monumental box which contained the works. The design was common enough, but the workmanship was most exquisite, and the clock was an excellent timekeeper besides, a matter of no small consequence in a land minus whistles, and gongs, and town clocks, and schools of children, and all the usual reminders of the lapse of time which shook in audible tones.

[25]

There, the wind murmurs through the foliage and makes light rustling sounds among the curtains. There, if you listen, you can hear the perpetual roar of the surf. There, the rattling of the coconut leaves, produces a sound like the pattering of fast coming rain. But all these sounds are continual. Only the great silent sun marks the hours, with dial fingers made of shadows.

After my husband had gratified himself by hearing my exclamations of satisfaction and seated me comfortably beneath the lace tent, he called the goddess Diana. That famous spirit appeared in the form of a negress, black, stout and comely, with gay turban, white corners to her eyes, and white teeth.[9] The sylvan goddess was now evoked for a breakfast.

"What have you got for us, Diana?" asked Pete.

"Coffee, turtle steaks, and waffles," replied the goddess, and expressed the hope that we had brought potatoes and crackers, for both were scarce.

Figure 12. This pen-and-ink drawing of Jenny Greenough's mosquito tent was probably done by Mannevillette Brown or his students (and nieces) Georgia and Villette Anderson. This full-page drawing was included within the pages of the manuscript. Courtesy of Jane and Raymond Gill and Elizabeth Traynor.

"Never mind crackers," said I, "get a loaf of bread."
"Bread, misses? I haven't time. I will try and make some by and by."

[26]

"Oh," said I, "I can make bread."
"How?" said my husband, with a comical look.
"Why?" I answered, "get some yeast —"
"Where?" he interrupted.
"At the grocer's," I replied.

At this the negress and he had a hearty laugh at my expense. Pete explained that yeast was not to be had in Key West, and that crackers were eaten as a substitute for bread, nor did they always have them. The population was so small, that a full cargo of any one sort of food, would glut the market, and for a while there would be plenty, but often no arrivals of provisions for some time, would deprive them of nearly everything but turtles. Of course I am speaking of Key West as it was long ago, what it is now, I know not.

That a young woman should be properly qualified to superintend a kitchen, and keep a house, was in the estimation of my mother, the only preparation necessary, to fit her to be married. In

[27]

that respect I was thought to be well educated. The text-book principally used in my instruction had been the American Housewife.[10] A very spreading name that, but it did not appear to have included the isles of the sea. My mother taught no first principles. Her teaching was entirely by example and experiment. I could cook almost anything New Englanders were accustomed to eat, but what was to be done with my learning, in a land where beef, mutton, veal, lamb, and chickens, were equally at a discount. A land where eggs were scarce, and milk was not to be had, except a little from goats. I remember on one occasion, some time afterward, being at a party there. Chicken salad was among the refreshments.

"Where did you get chickens?" I inquired.
"Young pork," whispered my friend.
"But the celery?" said I.
"Cabbage," replied the lady with a merry twinkle in her eyes.

Diana knew how to cook turtle, stewed, fried, or in soups. She could make delightful

[28]

waffles, and all manner of nice cakes, and was accustomed to keeping the house in perfect order. So finding my education would have to be learned all over again, I made haste to forget it, as young men do their college studies.

Pete left me, after breakfast, to attend to matters of business. What with examining my house, unpacking, arranging, and fighting the mosquitoes, I had enough to do the rest of the day. When evening was come, I was tired, and glad to rest upon the piazza, waiting for Pete to come home. As the moon rose, I saw for the first time the view of which I promised to tell you. The pillars of the piazza made a framework, through which I looked. There was the great ocean, stretching far away from eastern to western horizon, interrupted only by a low white bank or cay, which I take to be the original Spanish word for these peculiar islands.[11] Along this expanse of water, floated vessels of all nations, builds and sizes. Two or three were

[29]

always in sight. One, perhaps in such a position that her sails were white with the reflected light of the moon, while of another the sails were all in shadow. Imagine these seen through openings in the dark outline of the foliage, the moonlit sea, the glancing sails in the distance, the white pillars to frame them in; and you have the panorama to which I had a perpetual ticket of admission.[12]

There are great storms in life, when we are borne through deep waters, helpless yet safe in the ark of our innocence. When we emerge therefrom into new scenes and circumstances, the recollection of these former events recedes in imagination, until they seem part of a former existence. Such are the pictures which now rush on my memory, as I look back upon the long past. But I cannot let you see it all. Words have painted for you my house and my garden, words shall tell you of my friends, and my home, but no words can paint the storm which arose in my soul, — the cloud no bigger than a man's hand, which overspread the whole sky of my life,

[30]

and ended in one terrific storm.

I may as well tell you now, while I linger on the piazza, what I afterwards discovered about Key West. The soil of the Key, such as it is, is composed mostly of the debris of shells, which in some parts has hardened into limestone. The inhabited part of the island covered a spot about a mile in diameter. This was Key West. When you take into consideration a certain caudal appendage, which enables geographers to state that the island is eight miles long—nothing said of its width—why then it is Thomson's Island.[13] Of course there were no large trees indigenous to the place, and all attempts at horticulture were difficult and expensive. But difficulty, and expense are not obstacles which look insurmountable to a wrecker, and upon this natural raft, or rather light-ship, were a variety of the most unique and tasteful developments of sailor ideas. In one instance the soil had been brought in boat-loads from Tampa, a distance of about two hundred and fifty miles.

[31]

Cuba, being nearer, was often resorted to, but I suppose the navigation in that direction was not so easy.

In another case, the garden had been floored over with a smooth preparation of lime, which had hardened to the consistency of stone. In this artificial rock, round holes had been left, through which came up all manner of tropical flowers and shrubs, of which I remember particularly the beautiful paño de ora.[14] The flooring had the effect to confine the moisture, and thus prevent the too rapid evaporation, which is one of the causes of the natural barrenness of the island. I often planted a flower and industriously and conscientiously watered it, and considered that it was the flower's duty to grow; but grow it would not. At last, one day, I thrust my hand into the soil to discover, if possible, that I could immerse my whole hand in it, but around the

[32]

root of my pet no drop of moisture lingered. I withdrew my hand dry. Alas, how many blessings thus wither in our paths, for lack of knowing how to treat them.

But all the inhabitants of Key West were not as ignorant as myself. I frequently saw them encouraging vegetation by watering, and as the vegetables took courage and grew, I concluded they knew how things should be done. This watering was a most troublesome process, since the only fresh water obtainable was from the clouds of heaven. No river takes its rise, or empties, within all its three miles of circumference. It may boast a brook navigable for a shingle.

Around my own home had been planted every tropical tree the soil would bear. They were not of that great altitude we see in Cuba and elsewhere, but what they had lost in height, was gained in shade and unique beauty of form. The cocoanut trees looked like gigantic bunches of

[33]

plumes, so short their trunks, so immense their foliage. The royal palm was stunted and rotund, showing that even a tree will lose its beauty, if placed in uncomfortable circumstances. And under the shade of the beautiful tamarind, I was sitting when Pete came home.

After that day, I had no time to practice Key West cooking, had I been so disposed. A variety of ladies and gentlemen called upon me, and it seemed to me I found abundant occupation in dressing myself, talking to them, and returning their visits. There is a frequency in newly established societies, which old communities lose, whatever else they may gain. Your new place presents individual specimens of all the cliques known to old ones, with here and there a nondescript, the result of this very heterogeneous amalgamation.

In Key West we had not only all classes of people represented, but all kinds of nationalities. There were Spaniards and Minorcans, — the former very particular to explain the difference.

[34]

There were English, Irish, Scotch, Yankees, Southerners, Creoles, and Conchs; persons supposed to have floated over from the Bahamas, as a conch cannot be drowned. The only kind there were not, seemed to be Key Westers.[15]

The women were, if possible, more diverse than the men. There was the Cuban lady, little, fat, and good-natured. There was the substantial farmer's daughter from New England, active, lean, and talkative. There were fashionable ladies from New York and other cities, and very flashy ones from everywhere. These all met and danced in common, and abused each other with charming cordiality.

There were no great folks in those days. An individual of that sort would not have been tolerated a moment. There were only rich folks, and "I can spend as much money as you," was the open boast. Poor Mrs. Potiphar would have gone mad among them.[16] There was sudden wealth in unaccustomed hands, without any leading example to imitate. When an ignorant, low-

[35]

bred man becomes wealthy, he boasts and blusters, and imitates his neighbors in building fine houses, gambling or drinking, as his particular idiosyncrasy may lead him. An ignorant, low-bred woman, has no such range of choice; her one idea of wealth is dress. Of the pleasures of gambling and drinking, few of them have an idea. When men envy one another they pick a quarrel and fight it out. When women envy one another, they backbite and snarl, and serve each other with little petty annoyances, so long as they are within hail of each other's distance. Moreover they do not like to lose sight of each other; for this feeling is strong as love, and is often mistaken for it. I have seen two people who could not bear to separate so great was their desire to quarrel. Who has not?

The amusement which supplied the place of ball, opera, and theatre, was dancing: the Spanish dance being the favorite style. The floating motion so suited to a warm climate was to me extremely fascinating. I like to move to music without violent exercise.

[36]

Among the ladies who called upon me, was one who impressed me more strongly than others, from the peculiar style of her beauty. She was undeniably handsome, a brunette with dark eyes, and finely chiseled features, but with a certain coldness in the expression. Her speech was the superlative of decorum, her manners the veriest[17] ice of propriety.

"How do you like my friend, Mrs. Cantwell?" impressed my husband, so soon as he learned that the lady had paid me her respects, which she did within two or three days after my arrival, but I remember she was not the first to call.

"Your friend reminds me of a frozen blackberry." I answered. "She is dark, cold, beautiful, and insipid."

Peter looked thoughtful.

This lady was from New York. She had a daughter there at school, and I remember she remarked in the course of conversation, that she intended to bring her to Key West. I ventured

[37]

the remark that it was a pity to take the child from school and from the influences of refined society.

We were not so arrogant as to speak of ourselves as society. We were people met accidentally in a strange place. We were on business—to make fortunes. We would amuse ourselves a little, finish our business, and return to society and civilization.

But Mrs. Cantwell was of opinion that no society, or want of society, could compensate for a mother's influence.

Somehow this speech of hers pricked my conscience. I had enjoyed the influence of a good mother. Perhaps I had not appreciated the blessing sufficiently. I felt as if I had been ungrateful. I had fancied a mother hated to part with her children, for the same reason that a child hated to part with its toys, because she liked them. That a mother's influence is good is certain, but does maternity make one so sure of doing right?

This lady was one of Pete's patients, and he was very attentive to her, considering the nature

[38]
of her ailments, which permitted her to walk out whenever she pleased, and do all other acts and things, which well people may, and of right ought to do. But then she was a model woman in all respects. Calling upon her one day, she entertained me with pretty talking, intended to convey an idea of her extreme attachment to her husband. She went every evening to meet him, when he was coming from business. She thought men should be made aware of the interest felt in them in their houses.

I was astonished to hear it hinted by a woman of the world — certainly a person who ought to know — that humble distrust of their own importance, was one of the weak places in men's character which required fortification. To a young lady situated as I was, there is apt to be but one man in the world. I wondered if Pete was that way inclined, and being of an imitative disposition, and not to be outdone in duty or devotion by any mortal creature. I thought I would just try the experiment of waylaying him at his usual hours of return.

Almost all our houses were surrounded with more or less shrubbery. There was a large

[39]
garden attached to mine, and a small one round the dwelling of Mrs. Cantwell. Between us was the street or road. Going from my house I generally passed hers. I should have mentioned before that we boasted a horse and a stable. One could not walk all day about a tub without fatigue, and although the island was not much larger, Pete's practice kept him busy. But horses and horseback riding were not much in vogue, and if I heard a horse at all, I always thought of Pete.

Now it happened one lovely moonlight evening, that Pete had been to visit someone in the upper part of the island, and I was expecting him home. I fancied I could tell the tramp of his horse's feet. I heard him coming. I ran out on the piazza, but I could not see him. I started in my meditated project of meeting him, and saw his horse fastened at Mrs. Cantwell's gate. I went on, thinking I would go in, and see if she were ill. As I approached, I heard Pete saying.

[40]
"She is a mere doll. I should as soon think of one as being jealous of a poodle."

"And if a dog receives the affection which I covet, I am jealous of the dog," replied Mrs. Cantwell.

"And a very great dunce you would be," I interrupted; "for dogs cannot interfere with human affections, and anyone who could be jealous of a poodle, must be always in romantic calamity."

I could perceive that this little speech of mine, caused a startled look to come into each face. Then she turned pale, and he blushed. But they bid each other good evening, and he walked home with me, leading his horse. How came I to come after him? was his inquiry. I told him. He frowned, and told me to "quit that." I was a child, she a woman. He hinted good-naturedly enough, that even if I were a woman, I would be in no way be of capacity to match with her, and any attempt on my part to imitate her doings was presumptuous. When a man wishes his wife to

[41]

think humbly of herself he should—count the cost.

I did not repeat the attempt to go and meet him, but passed my evenings alone, walking up and down the piazza, enjoying the cool evening air, or dreaming away under my net. Sometimes I was lonesome. I thought my husband might contrive to spend an evening with me, now and then, but I considered that his business was of that nature, which would not permit to him any selfish disposal of his time, and I accused myself of folly and unkindness. So I went on building my little castle, out of my one anticipation of the time coming, when, the money made, we should go to Europe on another long voyage, as pleasant as the one which brought us there. Evening after evening passed this way, and week after week.

On one occasion, I thought I would slip off, and pay a visit. A lady is never quite up to the mark in her dress. It is reserved for gentlemen to reach perfection and be satisfied therewith. I

[42]

was standing before the glass putting a few extra touches to my apparel, when Pete tapped me on the shoulder, saying,

"What are you beautifying for, Madam Jenny Greenough?"

"I thought I would go round to Judge Crosby's," said I. "I have been frequently invited to come there in the evening —"

"What? And leave me alone!" was Dr. Peter Greenough's astonished reply.

"Certainly not," I answered, "if you will pass the evening with me, no company could be more agreeable, but I think when you have engagements elsewhere, it might be better for me to see company and dance, than to sit alone and mope."

"I did not think you missed me," he replied, and seemed to be pleased. He did not go out that evening, neither did I; but that old demon of excessive desire to please, destroyed me, I know, for he did not remain at home, the next evening, nor the next, nor the next for a great many

[43]

evenings. However I made no more attempts to go out, and the habit of solitary reverie I was forming, was fast rendering all society insipid to me.

We had a mail about once a month, and its arrival was of course a great occasion. With my little pile of letters and papers beneath my lace tent, my husband beside me, discovering the news of the great world in general, and our own little corner of it in particular, I was very content, entertained good opinions of things in general, and picked up new subjects of interest for my evening reveries. There is little sensible change of seasons in these ocean surrounded islands. It seemed, instead of summer and winter, to alternate between calm and storm; for I noticed in the conversation of almost everyone allusions to "the storm."

"What storm?" I asked.

"Oh, The Storm. We have a storm every Fall, a fearful storm," was ever the reply.

This one terrible storm to come every year, seemed to be the superstition of the island, and it

[44]

mingled largely in my imaginings. The hard work I prepared for poor Pete, and the desperate situations I contrived ways and means for him to get me out of, would be regarded as instances of the unreasonableness of women, if I were to write them out, therefore I say nothing more of my reveries.

One morning, letters informed us of the arrival in New York of my sister and her husband from Europe. My brother-in-law was a man of property, but not wealth. He was understood to wish for some slight employment. My husband told me, he thought of advising him to get himself appointed Insurance Agent. I think I must explain the nature of that office, and its expediency, for such as may be curious in the matter, premising that it has no leading connection with my story.

There are two sorts of wrecking, to which vessels are liable, among the gulf keys. There are pure wrecks, which occur in calms and storms, when the worthiest sailor has no power to control

[45]

the forces around him, and there are wrecks when the excellent Captain has his instructions, and the consignee and wrecker know beforehand where it will take place. These latter sort are generally in imitation of the doings of calms. It is not easy for me, not initiated, to distinguish the pure, from the bogus, wrecking. The reader will perceive that this sort of rascality, is altogether another matter from piracy as wrecking is elsewhere understood. The cargoes of these vessels were made up expressly to be wrecked. A lot of linen, calico, sewing cotton, toweling, and such things of use everywhere; goods accidentally damaged, from auction, picked up cheap anywhere, were shipped, and duly cleared for some port, which obligated the vessel to pass that way, say for South, or Central America, New Orleans, or Tampa. On a certain day some wrecker will go up into the observatory, glass in hand, will look seaward towards a certain quarter, when

[46]

he suspects a wreck may have occurred and behold, it is there, sure enough. Or he may sail away some fine morning, and meet with similar luck. It is wrecker law that the first comer should be the one employed. So of course one can perceive that it is necessary to keep a sharp lookout, and if one knows of a wreck about to be, he must be alert, and not let his left hand know what his right hand doeth.

After a wreck one may see the cargo piled up heterogeneously upon the wharves, in wet, bedraggled and uncouth looking heaps; whence they are knocked off at ridiculously low prices, under the auctioneer's hammer, to the various mob of sailors, shop keepers, fishermen and speculators, who throng to the sale. Then they are strewn all over the town for drying. I have seen the housetops white with linen, so that one, looking there, might have fancied it a fresh fallen snow; and the fences fashioned with cloth, until regarding them, one would think it a gala day.

[47]

And so the insurance companies which are very suspicious corporations and cunning withal,[18] kept an agent there, whose business it was to keep his eyes and ears open. This was the office Pete proposed for my sister's husband, that we might have the pleasure of their society. Upon this hint he spake, and obtained the situation. Finally it was arranged that they were to come out and live with us, and we were to be very rich, and very happy, thereafter forever.

This arrangement excited me a great deal. I felt a desire to talk about it continually, so I went round among my neighbors, and informed every one of my good luck. They all congratulated me, and some commended her sisterly affection in coming to such an out of the way place to dwell with me. Among others I told Mrs. Cantwell. She was particular in her inquiries about my sister. Her appearance, her size, the color of her hair and eyes; her style, if she were beautiful or fascinating; her age, her wealth, all appeared to interest her. I had not seen her for three or four

[48]

years, but I reported her as being a miracle of beauty and fascination.

"Is she like you?" she inquired.

"No, my very opposite. I have dark hair and eyes, my sister is a curly haired blond." In due course of time, that sister arrived, magnificent in New York and Parisian finery. She was indeed beautiful, but if she had not been so, that condition would only have furnished additional exercise for her talents. Not a ribbon, not a flower, not an ornament, or contingent article, was suffered to be on her person, but its effect on her particular style, was the study of a glance, and its proper arrangement, the work of an instant. She did these things with perfect openness, and the expressed intention of being as charming as possible. She was very lively, full of anecdote, description, and repartee, she danced and sang, and played upon a harp, which she brought with her, and chatted in half a dozen different languages. In short, she was superlative and Mrs. Cantwell was no where. I was both amused and enlightened, at the effect she produced.

[49]

Pete's patients recovered wonderfully. Sometimes for a week, no one would require his services, throughout the evening hours. I was glad to have my home made attractive, and sorry I had not myself the power to render it so. I could not help it, that I was not as beautiful, as artful, and as travelled as my sister; neither did see how I was to remedy these defects.

Now recurred to me the meaning, of being "too young." I could perceive that I was not a companion to my husband. I was simply a pet. I loved him, and he loved me; but it was my sister who kept him from Mrs. Cantwell's. It was my sister who took him to task for gambling. I had not perceived that he had that vice. It was my sister who dared to rate him soundly if he did not attend properly to his business. She it was, who could suggest to him and to her own husband, plans which interested, and give information which gratified them. All this ought to have been gratifying, and everybody congratulated me, but I felt somehow left out, and in the

[50]

wrong place. I found myself dreaming away about the sort of person who could love me, and I would check myself, feeling guilty, as if I were loving another, and that other not my liege lord.

There was a light-house upon the island and I frequently made that locality, the end of a ramble, upon which occasions, I used to rest awhile at the dwelling house of the family who kept the light.[19] There was one Don Joaquin Soldano, an old Spanish gentlemen, brother of the light-house keeper's wife, who had a son, also named Joaquin, at school somewhere north. I frequently sat on the piazza and talked with him, and he used to read to me his son's letters, with great pride and satisfaction, calling him all the time "el muchachito," "el jovencito," "el pequeño."[20] This boy, child, and youngster, was older than myself by two years. One day the conversation turned upon getting married. I was beginning to think it a great misfortune for any one to marry, so slim was the chance of marrying to content oneself. So I hoped that Don Joaquin's son would not get married "yet awhile." This was not so very absurd, as the old

[51]

gentlemen seemed to look forward with pleasure to such an event, but they laughed at me.

"Why do you laugh?" I said. "I am married and I am but sixteen."

"Oh," replied Mr. Mansfield, the lighthouse keeper, "women mature much younger than men."

"It seems to me, we women never have a chance to mature," I answered. "It is the fashion to take us from school at sixteen and seventeen, and set us about getting married, whereas boys of the same age are put at school, trade, or business, and the hardest kind of study."

"How would you like that?" said Mr. Mansfield.

"Much," I declared.

They laughed again. Mrs. Mansfield asserted that it would have been hard to make her study, when she was of my age.

"And I am like you," said her son Philip.

This youth's years numbered twenty-two.

[52]

He was a robust, fine-looking young fellow, and evidently intellectual, if not a student.

Mrs. Mansfield had several children. There were two girls called respectively, Priscilla Amanda, and Lodowiska Penchita Joaquina. Besides Philip, who seemed to have been christened while his sponsors took breath, for his name was simply Philip, there were two boys, Neptune Solon Junius, and Eusebio Constantio Claudio. It does me good to write down the very luxurious names, in which people sometimes indulge themselves; and in which Florida used to abound. Mr. Mansfield was a Yankee, and his wife a Spaniard. Mr. Mansfield was a man of method also. He would give one child an English name, and the next one a Spanish name alternately, as they were born. This he did because he thought it strict justice between his own and his wife's language. But, like many another ignorant person, he missed his mark in a way he

[53]

did not suspect, for he made the names all English by his fashion of pronouncing them. It was scarcely possible to observe proper decorum, when he called out "Load-o'-Whisky Punch-eater Walk-in-er,["] in his loud distinct way as if scorning the affectation of mincing sounds.

To resume our conversation:

"It would be hard for you to study from books, Philip. Knowledge gets into the head of such as you without study," said Mr. Mansfield.

"Different persons require different treatment," added Mr. Soldano.

"Then," said I, "I wish I had been a different person."

"Why?" said Philip.

"Because I wish I knew something."

"Why don't you read?"

It was not easy for me to answer this question, for I did read. It seemed to me reading did not answer the purpose. I was silent. Mr. Mansfield here told one of the children to "bring another bottle from the portfolio."

[54]

I looked after the boy rather wonderingly, expecting to see some juggler's trick produced for my amusement; but he took the desired bottle from an old fashioned beaufet.[21]

At this moment Mrs. Mansfield happily asked me,

"Do you want some stockings?"

"What size?" I inquired.

"Eights," she answered. "My feet are smaller than the girls, so I have taken a gross for myself, but I don't need so many."

Having negotiated for a portion of the stockings, I remarked that I would like some linen and thread, of which I had heard there had been some wrecked. I was informed that there was a lot for sale in the loft over Mr. Cantwell's store.

Soon after I returned home. As I neared my house, I was accosted by Mrs. Cantwell who

[55]

informed me that she and my sister were intending to go down and look at the same lot of goods; and I volunteered to accompany them. A vessel had been wrecked loaded with dry goods, which goods were displayed in a loft over Mr. Cantwell's store, previous to being sold at auction. When there was a wreck of dry goods, everybody traded. The goods could not of course be sold in retail quantities, so the ladies were given a chance to look at them, and the gentlemen bought them at auction; and then there would be an exchanging, dividing, and bartering among all the women in the place. Then my sister and Mrs. Cantwell would bestir themselves, give orders to their respective husbands, and thereafter divide the goods with the most amiable animosity. They hated each other, but that did not prevent them from treating each other with perfect good breeding. This was edifying to me, as showing how women, as well as men, can suppress their feelings for the sake of their interests.

[56]

Thus my life flowed on, and would have been pleasant enough, but for a certain restraint which grew up in my heart whenever I was in my husband's presence. I thought that I was not all his heart desired, and this feeling became at last so powerful that it caused me to avoid him. In vain I strove against it. The more I endeavored to love him, the more impossible it became. My opinion of him was not changed, but I felt that he did not love me. Under the influence of this feeling, my heart turned to my childhood's home. I longed to see my mother's face, to hear my father's cheerful voice. I thought of the pleasant days passed all so unreflectingly, when no coldness repulsed my desire for sympathy, when the possibility of a diminution in any one's love for me, had never passed through my mind.

One evening we were looking over the balcony, watching a large steamer coming in when

[57]

my brother-in-law came up and announced his intention of going in her to New York.[22] I wished that I could go also and pay a visit to my mother, not much heeding what I said.

My husband caught at the idea and my sister approved of it. They thought it would be good for me. She would keep house. They hurried me off to get ready, while Pete went down to the steamer and ascertained that she would remain in port several hours. Somehow I felt surprised. I earnestly wished to see my mother, that was certain, but I hated for them to be so very willing to part with me. However there was no time for reflection, as the steamer only stopped to take the mail. My trunks were hurriedly packed and carried down to the wharf.

The entire town at such times gathered upon the one wharf of the Key. In the darkness and crowd, it was impossible to find porter or servant, and my husband actually carried my trunks on

[58]

board himself, for fear I should be left behind. Surely the very demon of ingratitude possessed me. I felt as if thanking him was irony. We all kissed each other and bid good bye in the most hurried manner, for there had been but just time enough to get ready and be off; and I found myself sailing away, very much to my own wonderment.

A crowded steamer is something to see, and sometimes something to have lived through. It was necessary when anyone wished a berth on the steamer, to send to Havana and engage passage some three weeks beforehand, or take one's chance when the vessel came along. My chance was none at all. I went down into the cabin with my brother-in-law. In the just sufficient lamp light, I could see that the entire floor was covered over with cots, so close to one another, as to leave but just enough space to walk between. Upon every one of these cots lay a human being, apparently asleep. All of them were in half undress, and most all were men. How odd they looked! Their coats off, their dark nether garments, white shirts, and black heads, gave

[59]

them the appearance of being in uniform. I observed two vacant spaces and was told these were the appointed resting spots of my brother-in-law and myself. I proposed that we should sit on deck awhile. On deck we went. It was a clear, starry, night, without moon, and the heavy black smoke of the steamer streamed way behind with its myriad of sparks. It was cool but not pleasant. There was semi darkness and a sleepy crowd everywhere. I stumbled at one poor fellow's head, trod upon another's hand, and, in my confusion, fairly sat down upon a third. It was clear there was "no spot in all the earth, save one, to shelter" me, so we fumbled and stumbled our way back to the cabin. There had been great buying up of pillows and blankets and whatever may be said about demand creating supply, I can vouch for it, that pillows were demanded importunately, and fabulous prices offered therefor, but no pillows were forthcoming. Why don't steamers carry pillows in great plenty as life preservers? Why could they not be made so as to be fastened on to the person at the shortest notice? It was the fashion, some years

[60]

ago, for ladies to puff out the sleeves of their dresses with feathers, and I have heard of instances of their lives being saved thereby, in the upsetting of boats. Pillows could be made to answer a similar purpose.

My brother-in-law was a tall, stout, red whiskered Englishman. He had always had plenty of money, and bought therewith plenty of comfort. He was vexed whenever he could not make the barter. The closeness of the cabin, and motion of the steamer, gave him a headache. I fixed him up a pillow out of his carpet bag, and comforted him so much that I think the inclination came over him to buy me, but reflecting that I belonged to the family, seemed to satisfy him, and with a compliment to my mother, as being a woman who knew how to raise daughters, he went to sleep.

I laid down on my cot, but found it impossible to sleep. There was not much sickness, for the ocean was quite smooth, but the closeness of the cabin was unpleasant. The clash of the

[61]

machinery and all the slight tickering[23] sounds, which came out so distinctly on a steamer by night, like the chirp of the crickets on land, seemed loud and wearisome.

Presently I heard a slight, very slight sound, differing from the usual ones. Every form in that sleeping crowd waked with a start. Some listened, some dressed but I had no time to observe, for I was forcibly seized, and in an instant carried on deck. I felt that the rush was tremendous, but I was borne along by some strange arm. At such times, the powers of our human intellect hint to us of what great things we may be some day capable. That I was not frightened was probably owing to my ignorance of the danger, but in a moment of time I saw, what in years of writing I could not relate. With one bound I seemed borne from my cot to the open air in the first rush of the startled crowd. As if from the very spot where I had lain, I was plunged into the ocean. There was a loud explosion, a fearful shriek. Instinctively I caught at

[62]

and clung to a piece of the floating wreck. Whoever saved me, lost me in the shock, but it was not my brother-in-law.

All around me in the darkness, were the floating pieces of wreck mingled indistinguishably with dark forms, shrieking, groaning, beseeching, helpless. Oh, how hard I searched with eyes and ears to discover my

Figure 13. Depicting the Greenoughs' house from the perspective of the front entrance looking out across the porch, this pen-and-ink drawing was probably done by Mannevillette Brown or Georgia or Villette Anderson and was included with the manuscript. Courtesy of Jane and Raymond Gill and Elizabeth Traynor.

brother-in-law, but he probably never awoke from that sleep in which he closed his eyes, while blessing my mother. I floated about holding on, but getting very tired, and stupidly weary. Simply the instinct of life saved me, for the thought actually occurred to me, as I held on to my life preserving bit of wood, that I might as well end my life there.[24]

Day dawned at last, and a ship came along. A boat came to our rescue. I remember being tenderly treated. Of the number on the steamer, there were but few saved. These crowded the

[63]

ship, which was bound for New York. The steamer's destination had been Charleston. Such as desired it, were transferred to vessels going in that direction, but I continued on to New York, glad to get so much nearer to my home, but wondering how I was to proceed. I told how I had been saved, and tried to discover who had been my preserver, but everybody had a story to tell. Every man had been a hero; and of the two or three women saved beside myself, one was handsome, and had escaped romantically some how, at which she was so pleased, she seemed ready to be blown up again. Another woman had lost all her money and her husband, and she bewailed each with loud fidelity. The third woman was a star. She behaved with the dignity and serenity of a Christian heroine, which she was. Nobody was proud enough of having saved me, to accept the thanks I begged permission to render, and at last I took the Christian woman's advice, and thanked my Father in Heaven. Since I had been saved from death by almost a

[64]

miracle, it seemed to me I was saved for some wise purpose and from the depths of my desolation, I began to learn to trust in God. I had no difficulty in procuring money, or friends. The Christian lady gave me advice and companionship, until I was fairly started for my mother's house.

I have little to tell of my visit home. My dear father was kind and cheerful as ever. He doubted if a Southern climate was good for me, I was so thin. My little brother and sister were taller, but had not outgrown their love for me. To my mother only, I fretted. She seemed to think I was in a morbid state of mind. And truly what had I to complain of? I had nothing to tell, and my mother warned me that nothing was worse for a young wife than to fall into discontent. With all tenderness, yet as if it were a duty, she hinted that a wife should never quit her husband.

I signified how willing my husband had been to part with me.

Figure 14. Jenny Greenough floating on flotsam. Included with the manuscript, this pen-and-ink drawing was probably done by Mannevillette Brown or Georgia or Villette Anderson. Courtesy of Jane and Raymond Gill and Elizabeth Traynor.

[65]

She had no doubt I had been moping, and thought he acted kindly.

I began to believe not only that I had married too young, but that an age when I should arrive at sufficient wisdom for the state of matrimony, would never be attained by me.

The saddest of my occupations was to write to my sister an account of the death of her husband, for dead I could not but believe him to be, although of course a doubt would remain for a few weeks, as the various possibilities of miraculous escape, with which hope combats despair, suggested themselves. But week after week passed, and no letter or tidings arrived to lend the fact the least shade of uncertainty.

I had been at home about a month when Joaquin Soldano paid me a visit, having been directed to do so by his father's letters. He was on his way home. I asked why he did not defer returning until after the storm.

That was the very thing he was going to see. He hoped the storm would not come off until

[66]

he should get there.

The idea pleased me. I determined to return also, taking advantage of his going to have an escort. My mother approved. She thought storms as likely to occur at one season of the year as another but a speedy return to a disconsolate husband, a thing which should not be put off. So this matter was arranged. I fancied I should arrive at home unexpectedly and thus give them an agreeable surprise, for I thought perhaps my mother was right, and pleased myself with the idea that I was loved and would be gladly welcomed, although I still believed I did not hold the right place in my husband's affections.

None but the most ordinary, steady old codgers of winds blew us along the coast on this my second voyage on the little yacht like thing, in which we took passage. The old Captain greeted me kindly, when I went on board, asking after my husband. After answering his questions, I

[67]

went on deck with Joaquin, to sit there as the vessel sailed out of the harbor. While watching the fast receding city, I heard someone singing an old patriotic Spanish song, to a wild martial air, altogether new to me. Joaquin looked startled, jumped up with boyish impetuosity, but again sat down. I asked what was the matter.

"I think I know that voice," he answered.

"Why don't you go and see who it is?" I said.

"I will," he replied and started off. After a stirring flourish, the voice ceased, and I saw Joaquin in conversation with a youth about whom there was a strangely familiar air.

"Smart youngster that," said the old Captain coming to the side of the vessel, and looking at me with the air of a man who has more to say.

"Who is he, and what has he been doing?" I inquired.

I must make a short story of the Captain's long one, which was so abundant in detail and

[68]

redundant in sea terms, that, strictly reported, I am afraid it would be unintelligible. Besides it was punctuated all through with tobacco expectoration which would be impossible to put down. The Captain said that the young man was a Key Wester, that a ship laden with sugar had been wrecked at the Key, and the cargo set up at auction. It may be as well to state that it was customary, when a wrecked cargo was sold at auction, to set up one barrel or bale, and bid it off. Then if the purchaser chose he could say,

"I take the cargo." In which case, he had the privilege of buying the whole cargo at the same rate as the first barrel or bale. This lad, a boy of good repute, attended the sale for the purpose of buying a single barrel for his father's family. In a small community like that, each individual knows all his neighbors. The men attending the auction would not outbid the youth, thinking him such a boy and willing that his family should have the barrel cheap. And he did get it cheap,

[69]

so cheap that he astonished the bystanders by "taking the cargo." He then went to the monied men of the place, and upon the strength of his bargain raised the money to pay for it. The old Captain being there at the time, the cargo was sent in his vessel to New York. But the young one started by steamer, was blown up, floated about on a friendly spar a day and a night, was picked up by a vessel bound to Charleston, whence he started for New York. There he met the Captain, sold the sugar, realized a large profit, and was now returning home, having placed the proceeds in bank, with the intention of paying therewith for a wrecker to be built in Connecticut.

When Joaquin came back he was accompanied by Philip Mansfield. So he was the singer, the "smart youngster" that was blown up.

"O Philip," I said, "were you on the steamer that night?"

He answered gravely that he was, and commenced to tell of the scenes he saw, and his day

[70]

and night's experience of floating on the waste of waters.

It was September, the fatal month. The Captain and Philip wondered we had not put off our return until after the storm. We replied that we had come purposely to see the storm.

"You may happen to see more than you bargain for," said the Captain.

I shudder now as I remember the flippancy with which we spake of that terrible event.

We three were the only passengers. We had delightful weather, we were returning home, and the young gentlemen were in fine spirits. Oh, how sweet were these lovely sunsets, those moonlit evenings when with anecdote, and song, and social chat and long scientific speculations, we would while away the hours far into the night, almost grudging ourselves the necessary time for sleep.

I remember when we were in the neighborhood of Abaco Island; the old Captain told us a story which illustrates the singularly provoking nature of the calms, which try the patience of

[71]

sailors in the peculiar navigation of this region. In going down the coast, it is usual to take advantage of the Gulf Stream. Our Captain hoped the same luck would not befall him, which had overtaken another of his calling. On one occasion two vessels cleared from New York, for New Orleans. One proceeded to its destination, discharged its cargo, and was on the return voyage when the other vessel was met, still near Abaco. It had passed the island three times, and each time, on quitting the Gulf Stream, encountered a calm which had drifted it back completely around the island. By this time the captain had become so enraged, that he had torn down his ratlines,[25] in order, he said, that his sailors might have work, and feel as bad as he did.

As we neared the end of our voyage, we were becalmed one day for three or four hours. We sat on deck watching sea and sky, and whistling for a wind. I noticed a little wrecker gliding

[72]

along, although we could not. I asked Philip the reason.

"They are modelled so as to be able to sail with very little wind," he answered; "and their bottoms are polished like a mahogany table."

"How is it that they can sail in shallow and deep water both?" I said.

"They have movable keels," he replied, "which can be lowered in deep water, and raised in shallow."

Suddenly there fell on our ears the low rushing sound made by the opposing wind and current. Far away, in the dim horizon, might be distinguished a long dark cloud. Immediately the wind swept the distant billows and crested them with foam. The liquid darkness, as it were, dissolved, and spread over half the sea. Gradually and regularly the little waves came on, and on, widening as they came and mingling and roughening the hitherto still waters around. The vessel feels the swell. She rocks, she rides the bounding waves. The Captain commenced

[73]

rapidly giving orders, and by the alacrity of every soul on board I knew something unusual was transpiring. Fortunately we were near our destination, and in a short time we were at the wharf.

Upon landing, Joaquin and Philip departed for their home, after leaving me at the gate of my garden. I crept up the long sandy path, towards the house, with my studied intention of surprising my friends. I expected they would be sitting upon the end of the piazza, or walking there to and fro, and almost fancied I could tell what they would be talking about. I drew near the house, but everything was silent. I walked in. The place had a packed up look. The net was removed, the windows were closed. The last rays of the setting sun breaking through the angry clouds streamed from the open door across the room. Suddenly I thought they might be ill or dead. I turned back towards the piazza, for I have said before, there were stairs upon the outside of the building. Half way up these stairs stood Diana shading her eyes with her hand, and

[74]

watching the vessels that were scudding across the water to places of safety. I called to her and asked, where were my husband and sister?

"Lor bress your soul, Missus," said she, coming down, "how come you here? Massa and Miss Melinda gone for meet you, till the storm be passed, but I tink de storm come now. Day went dis mornin. May de Lord take care of dem. Missus I go get you some tea."

"No," I replied, "I want no tea, but go and get some one to bring my trunk up."

"Yes, Messus," she answered, and started on her mission.

I went back into the parlor and sat down. It was getting dark, and the wind kept shaking the glasses and doors after a dismal fashion. I felt very lonesome and unhappy, and caught myself wishing Philip would come and see me. Then I felt as if there were something very wrong, and absurd, in my wishing he would come, but I knew that, except such as might learn the

[75]

fact that evening, no one on the island could be aware of my return. Diana now entered, saying,

"I brought you some tea, Missus, and some waffles, and a bit of tongue. You must eat suffin, for dere's no tellin but we be blown away 'fore mornin. Guess we hab de storm now."

I drank and ate and was refreshed and grateful. Diana left me a light but the wind soon blew it out. At this moment I heard a step on the piazza, and Philip Mansfield came in. He said he had heard that my husband and sister had left, and had come to offer me his services. I thanked him, thinking his offer one of general politeness merely, and after a few minutes chat he departed.

The wind had now risen to a perfect howl. I looked out of the window. The clouds were driving along in great black masses overhead. The sea looked dark and angry and every wave

[76]

was capped with a white crest of foam. The cocoanut trees bowed their great branch-like leaves to the very ground. The extraordinary height of the waves, dashing in far beyond their usual limits, amazed me. One arose so high and dark, I trembled to look at it. It drew near, broke, sweeping away fence and trees, and spreading its white foam half way up the garden. I was so anxious and dismayed that I could not help wishing I had by some means held on to Philip, who had evidently called in pure compassion for my helpless situation, and his sailor-like foreknowledge of the coming storm. In such an hour, how we value the companionship of the brave and strong. In my distress I thought aloud,

"I wish he had stayed."

I thought I heard a voice very near me say, "He did." I turned to look around. The room was in the blackest darkness. At that moment the wind burst in with a great crash, doors and

[77]

windows broke open, glasses smashed. The furniture dashed across the room, and the spray and rain rushed in my face, telling me the surf had reached the house. Two strong arms were thrown around me, and I felt myself borne along uninjured amid all this wild commotion, into the open air. The broken fragments of trees and buildings all tossed about, made great confusion in the dark night. The noise was so great we made no attempt to speak. A speaking trumpet could not have been heard at three yards distance. I clung to my protector. The sea had washed up on the island, and wading through in the softened soil, I lost both shoes and stockings. My clothes were literally blown off me. I must have been blown away myself, as a mere feather, but for the strong man who alternately lifted and sustained me, until, past houses and past danger, he sat me down in the Storm House, a place of safety built on the highest part of the island, for just such an emergency as this. The building was of one story, constructed of the most solid materials, fastened to the ground by iron bolts or other strong clamps, and farther made secure against the

storm, by being strengthened, like a ship, with knees[26] and timbers.

Here we met plenty of company already assembled. What a forlorn set we were, with our feet bare, our clothes torn, our hair hanging wet upon our shoulders, for combs were nowhere. Of course it was dark. By voices and by questions we endeavored to ascertain who were there and who were safe. I think we could have been merry, but for the intense anxiety for the fate of those we missed. Meantime the night wore on. We made frequent attempts to light bits of candle, but they gave but small light, flaring in the wind and ever and anon being blown out. Among the persons there, I found several friends. Mrs. Cantwell was there, and wondered at my returning just then, but did not appear to have learned of the departure of my husband and sister. When I told her, she remarked that the only vessel which had left the harbor that day had been

bound for England. "However it can't make much difference," said she, "for even the ships in the harbor will not be able to stand this." Started for England! What thoughts that information suggested to me. But I had learned to think and not speak. Meantime the hours passed on.

Towards morning the storm lulled, and such of the families — of which there were but few, as had not had their houses blown down, or cleaned out, sent us garments and invitations to breakfast. Among others, a gentleman brought from his store a box of shoes. What was my amazement to see a scramble for fits, and one lady refused to wear any of them. They were all too big. Well, I have said before that I had given myself up for a dunce, but it did seem to me at that moment that there were greater fools in the world than myself. From the clothes which the wiser ladies had rejected, I selected a garment which I believe sailors call a pea jacket although

what idea associates it with a pea, I cannot tell. It was very thick and warm, and I felt comforted by it, but I am afraid it was very ungraceful. I had tied a pair of shoes to my feet, which, I think, weighed two pounds each, and which I calculated covered area sufficient to prevent me from slumping in the softest sand. My long wet hair was streaming down over my jacket. I was sitting upon a bench, my elbows resting on my knees and my chin on my hands, thinking, wondering what I was to do. Where were my friends? Had I friends? Oh, in my heart, how lonesome I felt. Some, whose friends were all safe, were very merry at my odd appearance, but I could not laugh; I was haunted with the thought of that vessel sailing out of the harbor. Were they safe?

After depositing me in this house, Philip Mansfield had departed to save other lives, if

[81]

possible, but he now returned to look after my farther welfare. I longed to speak all the gratitude and admiration, with which my thoughts were filled, but the intensity of my emotions was so great, and seemed so little in harmony with those around me, that I felt restrained. Philip too seemed exceedingly sorrowful, scarcely able to speak. Poor fellow! In his anxiety for my safety, or rather in quitting his home, he had saved his own life. His family, for greater security, had all taken refuge in the lighthouse. Fatal mistake! The lighthouse had been swept away. Joaquin, Mr. Soldano, father, mother, brothers, sisters, all were gone.[27] What words of consolation could I utter?

At this time I was rejoiced to see Diana arrive. She came with an invitation to breakfast from Judge Crosby's family. His house was a substantial building located near the Storm House, and there had Diana found shelter during the night.

[82]

"Laws a mercy, Missus, how you look! but I found your trunk, and Missus Crosby send you a shawl."

To Mrs. Crosby I went, but Philip could not be persuaded to enter the house. He rushed off in the direction of the sea, leaving me full of anxiety on his account. Dear Mrs. Crosby insisted upon preparing rooms for both of us. She had been preparing a number of nice new quilts, and had stowed them snugly away in her attic, against the needs which might arise in the coming winter. Now, in this sudden call upon her hospitality she went up to fetch them, but upon putting her head through the door, to her amazement, she found the roof gone, and the garret swept of quilts and everything else.

All that day Philip returned not. I hoped the night would bring him, but night fell, and Judge Crosby came home and still we neither heard from nor saw him. I went to bed but not to rest. Fatigued as I was, I slept, but my sleep was startled with terrific dreams, and when the morning

[83]

came, I was in a state of wretchedness which would not permit me to rest. My friends shared my anxiety, and dear Mrs. Crosby proposed that the Judge and I should go in search of Philip, and persuade him to return with us to her house. How I loved her for the proposition. Had she not made it, I think I must have started out alone, however wild the thought might be, or however fruitless my endeavor to do him good. We were not long in making our preparations, and excited as I was, I think I could have found strength to walk a hundred miles. We mutually expected to find him in the neighborhood of his former home.

The way was not perfectly easy. In some places the island was a desolation, fences and streets were obliterated. Here and there a building was standing, roofless or windowless as the case might be. Fragments of houses and furniture, uprooted trees and various indescribable

[84]

rubbish were scattered in every direction. Of my own house the walls were standing, but it was an utter wreck. We passed on to the place where the lighthouse had been; its very foundations were gone. It was difficult to believe there had ever been a building on the spot. Still we saw nothing of Philip. I hated to quit the shore, and could not keep my eyes from the distant sea. My thoughts would stray to that vessel said to have gone to England. Gone to Europe! My dreams *thus* realized! Then the awful thought that not England, but that bourne whence no traveler returns, had been their destination. Beyond the light-house there had been a graveyard, and on we went, each alike impressed with the idea, that the state of Philip's mind would lead him in that direction. Dismal indeed was the sight we encountered. The headstones were all blown out of their places, some far up among the underbrush; but most horrible of all, the very dead had

[85]

been found forced from their graves, and in some instances the corpses were entangled with their grave clothes in the trees and shrubbery around.[28] My soul sickens at the recollection of those sights, which yet at the time I could not quit, until we should find the object of our search.

Far away up the beach there seemed to be a wreck, and thither we pressed on, as the most likely place of all to find our wanderer. As we drew near, we could perceive pieces of the wreck strewn upon the shore. A strange, sickening sensation almost suffocated me, as I beheld them. In my impatience to advance, my limbs seemed made of lead. I strained my eyes with such an intense wish to see, that they appeared to lose their power of distinguishing. I slipped my arm from the friendly support of the Judge, and started forward at a run. A mass of the shelly rock, which forms the foundation of the island, stretched out into the sea a short distance before me, and jammed among them was what I took to be part of a mast or spar. Resting upon this,

[86]

and bound to it, there seemed to my fascinated gaze, a female form, just sufficiently lifted above the water for the long hair to float away on the surface, and the white clothing moved by the water to envelope and conceal the limbs. I scrambled with slipping feet and torn hands, from rock to rock. I reached the spar. I endeavored to step upon it. The pressure of my foot on the wood caused a motion of the water, a portion of the shawl floated away, and there lay the pale dead face and arm of my own beautiful sister. I sunk down upon the rocks. I had consciousness enough to know that Philip and Judge Crosby came to my aid, and took me home. On arriving I was carried to my room and my dear friend and tenderest of nurses, Mrs. Crosby endeavored to sooth and console me.

Meantime Philip acquainted Judge Crosby with the fact, that he had convinced himself, that

[87]

the shipwrecked vessel was the one in which my husband and sister had sailed and that he had found his dead body upon the beach, not far from hers. Both had evidently been lashed to the spar to prevent being washed overboard. This intelligence was communicated to me as gently as possible, but coming after all my fatigue and excitement, it threw me into a fever from which I did not recover for many weary weeks. In the first stages of my sickness, I was delirious, in the latter very weak; but during all, my friends nursed me with the most tender kindness, and I had the inexpressible gratification of being told that care for my welfare had probably been the salvation of Philip. In his great interest for me, he was drawn away from his own griefs. Certain it is that he was ever ready to assist, or amuse, or aid me, in any way in his power.

[88]
One day when he seemed very sad, I felt an intense desire to say something consoling to him. As I could think of nothing else, I began to pour out my gratitude to him for having twice saved my life.

"Twice?" said Philip.

"Yes, twice," I replied, "for the same arms which saved me in the storm, were those which rescued me from the cabin of the steam-boat. There could not be two. I knew it when you bore me through the storm. I am not mistaken."

Philip was evidently gratified at this discovery of mine. He had never boasted of his heroic act, but I had told the Judge and Mrs. Crosby all about it.

Meantime letters came from my father, telling that my husband had written, bidding me not to return to Key West, as he had given up his practice, and intended to leave. The letter of course had been received after my departure. My father was as yet in doubt whether I had

[89]
arrived in season to see him before he left. I wrote to my parents that they had indeed left, were shipwrecked and dead, but the fatal truth, that they had started for England, instead of New York, I never mentioned, and have good reason to believe they never knew it.

As soon as my health was sufficiently recovered, I returned to my early home. Philip accompanied me to my father's house, but he never returned to Key West. Under the advice of my father, he went into business, and was very successful. In after time, when cheerful events and reading, and study, had softened into sad remembrances the terrible catastrophes of that night of storm, Philip and I were married. I had the pleasure of travelling with him in various lands, and never had occasion to believe that any other charm was greater to him than my own

[90]
influence. Whereupon I have concluded that perhaps I found at last the "proper time to marry." That time arrives when we can understand that sorrow is not romance, and that deep and strong affection is found only in sensible and stable persons.

Notes

1. William Cowper, "Pairing Time Anticipated, Moral" (lines 64–65).
2. Bracketed numbers indicate pagination as it appears in the manuscript.
3. See Exodus 8:20–24.
4. Variant of *eccentric*, still in common usage during the nineteenth century (*The Oxford English Dictionary,* hereafter *OED*).
5. See Genesis 49: 8–9.
6. Probably the narrator's misspelling of "Ligustrum."
7. While there are several vines with blue flowers, such as the morning glory, that can grow in the Florida Keys, there is apparently none with this name.
8. Obsolete variant spelling of "chimneys" (*OED*).
9. Like most other Black people in Florida, Diana would have been an enslaved person. As Maureen Ogle points out, "In the mid 1800s, Key West's 'fairy atmosphere'—and the nation's comfortable prosperity—rested on the backs of slaves, four hundred at Key West and four million in the nation. Key West whites hunted sponges and wrecks rather than ever-larger cotton fields, but ideologically and politically, most aligned themselves with the powerful slave-owning plantation minority on the Florida mainland and in the Deep South" (52). The Brown sisters also shared the views on slavery held by those in the southern society surrounding them. When they moved to Florida in 1835, it was a territory with slavery, and it became a slave state in 1845; also, they married men who were raised in slave states. In their letters, neither sister expresses interest in abolition, they never raise objections to slavery, and they seem comfortable with having "servants" about whom they sometimes complain. Ellen engages in a long-term epistolary debate with Mannevillette, who held much more progressive views than hers. In a letter of August 1, 1836, she tells him, "Your idea of slaves . . . is dramatically opposed to truth," and she shares with him the typical views of southern slaveholders concerning the inferior behavior not only of slaves but also of uneducated free Black people. She adds, "All this . . . necessarily follows from their situation in society, and until that is changed will continue so" (Denham and Huneycutt 39).
10. *The American Housewife: Containing the Most Valuable and Original Receipts in all the Various Branches of Cookery; and Written in a Minute and Methodical Manner Together with a Collection of Miscellaneous Receipts, and Directions Relative to Housewifery* (New York: Collins, Keese & Co., 1839). By 1851, the authorship of this book was attributed to Experienced Lady, and by 1853, it had gone through eight editions.
11. A key, or *cay* (Spanish), is "a low insular bank of sand, mud, rock, coral, etc.; a sandbank; a range of low-lying reefs or rocks; originally applied to such islets around the coast and islands of Spanish America" (*OED*). The origin of the name has been much debated, but this concise explanation by the online *Encyclopedia Britannica* seems the most plausible and widely accepted: "The name is an English corruption of *Cayo Hueso* ('Bone Islet'), the name given to it by Spanish explorers who found human bones there"; see https://www.britannica.com/place/Key-West

12 Panorama: "A picture of a landscape or other scene, either arranged on the inside of a cylindrical surface, to be viewed from a central position (also called *cyclorama*), or unrolled or unfolded and made to pass before the spectator, so as to show the various parts in succession. Hence, more generally: any pictorial representation of a panoramic view" (*OED*). For an extended discussion of this once-popular art form, see Stephen Oettermann's *The Panorama*.
13 This remark could refer to Thompson's Island in Boston Harbor.
14 Lantana.
15 This is an accurate description of Key West's diverse population at around 1850. When Spain sold Florida to the United States in 1821, Key West was a small, isolated island town that, due to its strategic location by the Florida straits and its deep port, steadily grew in size and importance during the next few decades. According to historian Canter Brown in *Ossian Bingley Hart*,

> Thanks to the economic stimulus provided by an influx of government money to rebuild lighthouses and military facilities, the population had grown to 2,645 in 1850, and Key West had become Florida's largest town.... The island's residents in the mid-1800s comprised a diverse lot. "It was a cosmopolitan population," explained an old settler, "Bahama wreckers and immigrants, small fishermen from Noank and Mystic, Conn., refugees from the mainland, gentlemen from Virginia, Georgia, and the Gulf States, business men, commercial adventurers and mechanics from the Northern States, and world wanderers from every portion of the globe." Included in the "rare aggregation" at various times were "Englishmen, Bahamians, Irish, Dutch, Swedes, Norwegians, Hindoos, Russians, Italians, Spaniards, Cubans, Canary Islanders, South Americans, Canadians, Scotch, French, shipwrecked sailors, deserters, and discharged men from the army, navy, and marine corps." (69)

Also, see *Echoes from a Distant Frontier*, 238–39.
16 See George William Curtis's *The Potiphar Papers* (1853). In this novel, which satirizes the pretensions of New York City society, Mrs. Potiphar is the superficial, younger wife of the main character.
17 Superlative form of *very*, meaning "really or truly entitled to the name or designation; possessing the true character of the person or thing named; properly so called or designated." This usage was still current in the nineteenth century (*OED*).
18 Archaic adverb meaning "in addition; besides; moreover; likewise; as well," but still current in the nineteenth century (*OED*).
19 The first Key West lighthouse, sixty-five-feet tall, was completed in 1925. According to Maureen Ogle in *Key West*, the hurricane of 1846 "toppled the lighthouse, killing fourteen people huddled inside" (42). A new lighthouse was built in 1848. The lighthouse received various improvements over the years but was deactivated in 1969 and now serves as a museum.
20 Spanish: "el muchachito"—"the little boy"; "el jovencito"—"the youngster"; "el pequeño"—"the small."

21   Alternate spelling of "buffet," still current in the nineteenth century, meaning "a cupboard in a recess for china and glasses" or "a refreshment bar" (*OED*).

22   Ellen and Corinna, along with other family members, frequently traveled by steamboat, including the Key West-Charleston-New York steamer, which Corinna describes to Mannevillette in a letter of November 22, 1849 (Anderson-Brown Papers). They often traveled on a "packet-boat," or "packet": "A boat or ship travelling at regular intervals between two ports, originally for the conveyance of mail, later also of goods and passengers; a mailboat" (*OED*). In a letter of May 6, 1849, written in New York City, Corinna tells Mannevillette that she, Ellen, Edward, and Virginia Anderson are taking a steamer to Key West (Anderson-Brown papers). On May 26, she writes again, saying that they have arrived. She mentions both the *Samson* and the *Isabel*, apparently both packets, and refers specifically to the *Isabel* as a steamer (*Echoes* 235–237).

23   Ticker: "Something that ticks" (*OED*).

24   The Brown family was familiar with the discomforts and dangers of steamboat travel. In a letter of December 22, 1849, Corinna described rough travel by steamship to New York. In a letter of March 8, 1950, George Brown wrote to Mannevillette that he was delayed in Charleston due to a steamboat wreck (Anderson-Brown Papers). Also, in a letter of July 17, 1851, Corinna told Mannevillette that Edward, in San Francisco at that time, was on the steamship *New World* when it blew up (Anderson-Brown Papers). On August 17, 1852, George wrote to Mannevillette about the disaster of the steamer *Henry Clay* on the Hudson River (Anderson-Brown Papers). As the boat raced another steamer, the boat's engine overheated and the furnace caught fire, killing more than fifty people; see "Dreadful Calamity of the Hudson River," *New York Times*, July 29, 1852.

25   Ratline: Any of the small lines fastened across the shrouds of a sailing ship like the rungs of a ladder, used for climbing the rigging. Frequently in plural (*OED*).

26   In shipbuilding, a "knee" is "a piece of timber naturally bent, used to secure parts of a ship together, esp. one with an angular bend used to connect the beams and the timbers; by extension, a bent piece of iron serving the same purpose" (*OED*).

27   This detail in the story was inspired by the tragic destruction of the lighthouse during the 1846 hurricane. Jay Barnes explains in *Florida's Hurricane History* that "the Key West Lighthouse, built in 1825 to a height of eighty-five feet, was swept away by the awesome tide, and with it fourteen of the keeper's family and staff" (60).

28   The graveyard scene is also based on accounts of the 1846 hurricane. According to Maureen Ogle in *Key West*, "A man investigating the damage there stumbled over graves 'wholly uncovered, and skeletons, and coffins, dashed about, and scattered far and wide.' The storm launched one coffin right out of its resting spot. It landed upright and leaned against a tree, its 'ghastly tenant looking out upon the scene of desolation around'" (42).

AFTERWORD

An Editorial Note on the Manuscript: Attributing Authorship and Tracking the Manuscript's Path

The unpublished, ninety-page manuscript of *The Storm* was donated to the P. K. Yonge Library of Florida History at the University of Florida in September 2015. According to Dr. Jim Cusick, special and area studies collections curator, the undated and unsigned story came with no verifiable provenance. Dr. Cusick contacted James Denham and me to explain that he had reason to believe that the manuscript was written by Corinna Brown Aldrich and Ellen Brown Anderson, or perhaps by Ellen alone, and he wondered if we knew anything about it since we had edited their personal correspondence. We were unfamiliar with the story, but because of the story's references to numerous aspects of life in Key West that resemble comments appearing in the sisters' letters written while they lived on the island in 1849 and 1850, and because of some similarities to other manuscript stories and fragments written by these sisters, the story appeared to be theirs. Unfortunately, the manuscript has no watermark, date, signature, or other definitive proof of the story's authorship or time and place of composition.[1]

The absence of the author's name on a nineteenth-century manuscript written by a woman and prepared for submission to a publisher should not be surprising. Women frequently adopted pseudonyms or remained anonymous when their writing was published, since writing generally was still not considered an appropriate occupation for women.[2] The two stories that the Brown sisters published in their lifetimes, Ellen's "A Novel in a Nut-Shell" and Corinna's "The Grumble Family," were unsigned, and the unpublished manuscripts still in the family's possession are nearly all unsigned or pseudonymous. When discussing with Mannevillette the writings that they intended to publish, they urged their brother to maintain the secrecy of their identities,[3] though Ellen sometimes signed her manuscript stories and essays "E.M.A.," her initials (Ellen Maria Anderson).

Dr. Cusick gave me a copy of another document included with the donated story, a typed introduction to *The Storm* by Norm La Coe, dated 1991, which pointed to the Brown sisters as likely authors. Mr. La Coe, an Alachua County historian,[4] had access to many of the Brown sisters' letters before Mike Denham and I had seen them, so it seemed reasonable to assume that he had good reasons for his belief, and his document indeed includes quotations from letters written by the sisters while they were in Key West and concludes with observations about the story and conjectures about its authorship. My own examination of both internal and external evidence supports Norm La Coe's belief that the Brown sisters probably were *The Storm*'s authors.

Mr. La Coe had since retired and moved from the area, but soon we struck up a friendly and productive correspondence related to *The Storm* and the letters. He explained that in the spring of 1972, Dr. Charles A. Hoffman Jr., a cultural anthropologist at the University of Florida, had invited him to participate in examining almost five hundred items of historical interest that had been brought to Gainesville. Most items in that collection were letters written to or from Brown family members living in Florida from 1835 to 1857, primarily siblings Corinna Brown Aldrich, Ellen Brown Anderson, and George Brown. According to Mr. La Coe, the manuscript of *The Storm* was included in that collection, a strong indication that *The Storm* was written by a member of this family. In a letter to me written on September 6, 2016, Mr. La Coe explained that, in 1972, "John Traynor showed up. . . . with an attaché case full of 500 or so old letters and the ms. to *The Storm*.[5] Eventually, I passed the letters on to Lewis Goolsby . . . and they eventually ended up purchased by a descendant[6] of Ellen Brown Anderson, who gave them to the library at West Point. I kept *The Storm* with Traynor's consent. . . . I ended up selling *The Storm* to a local rare book dealer. . . . At that time, the U. Fla. library told me they had no interest in it."

My correspondence with Mr. La Coe focused on the letters included in the Traynor Collection and on the manuscript of *The Storm*. When Mike Denham and I visited Mr. La Coe in the summer of 2017, he shared further information concerning the Traynor Collection that was taken to Gainesville in 1972, and he generously gave me various typed documents, manuscripts, and photocopies of letters in a large envelope labeled "John Traynor Correspondence."[7] These letters document the physical location of the collection, the distribution of photocopies, and the sale of family letters to Mr. Louis Goolsby in 1975. The original provenance of the letters in the Traynor collection is easily determined since all are dated and signed, with the location of the writer and the intended recipient and destination included. After arriving in Florida in 1972, the letters moved in several directions, but most can be easily tracked.

The path of the manuscript of *The Storm* can also be traced from its arrival in Gainesville in 1972 to its return to Gainesville in 2015, as I have done above. However, because *The Storm* was neither signed nor dated, other external and internal evidence is necessary to determine its provenance prior to its arrival in Gainesville in 1972. Since the manuscript was included with the family letters, that it was written by one or more members of the family seems obvious. Another safe assumption is that the author was intimately familiar with mid-nineteenth-century Key West, which would narrow the possibilities to Edward Aldrich, Corinna Brown Aldrich, and Ellen Brown Anderson, the family members who lived in Key West. The Traynor collection included letters written in Florida by George Brown, Ellen and Corinna's younger brother, and James Anderson, Ellen's husband, but these two men never saw Key West. The story's protagonist and narrator is a woman, and though it is possible that Edward could have written the story, he never showed any interest in writing fiction and not much interest in writing letters, while Corinna and Ellen both had literary ambitions and spent a good deal of time writing letters, stories, and essays. Other biographical and thematic evidence points to these sisters as the authors, so it is helpful to understand how the manuscript would have journeyed from the nineteenth-century author(s) to John Traynor.

When Corinna died in 1854, her personal effects, including letters or manuscripts, would have gone to Ellen, her closest relative. When Ellen died in 1862, Mannevillette, the oldest and last-surviving of the siblings, took her daughters, Georgia and Villette, back with him to Utica, New York. Will, Ellen's oldest child, was a cadet at the U.S. Military Academy at West Point, so the family papers would have gone with the girls and their belongings to Utica. These papers included the numerous family letters saved by Ellen and Corinna and manuscripts of various essays and stories, most—if not all—of which Ellen had written. Will, who had resigned from West Point and joined the Confederacy, had moved to Washington, D.C., by 1870, and his sisters soon left their uncle to join him and his wife, Lizzie, in Washington. That Ellen's collected papers remained with her daughters is verified by Villette's comment in a letter to Mannevillette on June 5, 1882, that she had just read a bag full of letters left to her by her mother. When Villette died in 1891, Ellen's letters and manuscripts, along with Villette's own saved letters, went to Will. To this growing collection, Will added those left by Mannevillette when he died in 1896. Will included his own letters in the family papers, and his wife, Lizzie, added a few, the last of which is dated October 22, 1899. According to surviving descendants, Will and Lizzie moved into a house on Chapin Street in Washington in 1903, taking the accumulated family papers with them. After Will Anderson died in 1915, the entire family collection of letters and manuscripts was stored for six decades in this house. Several of Will's unmarried children stayed in the Chapin Street house, including George Anderson, who remained until his death in 1968.[8]

In a letter to Norm La Coe dated May 6, 1972, Mr. Traynor, whose wife, Betsy Meyer Traynor, was George Anderson's great-niece, explained how he had assumed "custody of the collection": after George Anderson's death, family members "were asked to clean out the house in Washington, D.C. at the request of the executors. All items of familial or sentimental value to relatives were passed on by the estate. . . . While rummaging through the old house I discovered numerous old boxes of papers, etc. ensconced in the basement. It was while examining this detritus that I discovered the letters, which had been preserved for so long, apparently by Uncle George's father [Will Anderson]."[9]

The contents from the Anderson-Brown family collection that John Traynor took to Gainesville in 1972 are well documented. Although the entire family papers consist of around nine hundred letters and other manuscripts, Traynor included in the selection that he took to Gainesville only those items directly related to Florida—still a considerable number. Surviving correspondence shows that he first displayed the collection to Dr. Charles Hoffman during the Easter vacation of 1972. Hoffman soon showed the collection to Norm La Coe and Louis Goolsby, a local philatelist. In a letter of October 12, 1972, Norm La Coe explained to John Traynor that Dr. Hoffman had moved to Arizona for a new teaching job and left the collection "in my care and custody." A letter from Louis Goolsby to John Traynor, dated February 25, 1973, says that the letters cover a thirty-year period "from 1821 [to] about 1860. . . . The collection includes between 480 and 485 letters, plus one or two additional documents from the same period." Goolsby, who was interested in the letters specifically for their philatelic value, did not identify the other document(s). Letters between Traynor and Goolsby reveal that Goolsby bought the Florida letters from Traynor in April 1975. One of the letters includes a complete list of the purchased items, but the manuscript for *The Storm* is not among them. As explained above, the manuscript for *The Storm* was part of John Traynor's collection, but, with Traynor's permission, Mr. La Coe kept it until he sold it to the rare book dealer.[10] Fortunately, taped to the box holding the manuscript is a card dated September 2015, identifying Alice and Gary Nippes as the donors, along with a business card for Gary Nippes Books: Art Books and Prints, with a Micanopy, Florida, address, about seventeen miles from Gainesville.

It was almost definitely O. J. Briskey, a bookseller in Micanopy, to whom Mr. La Coe sold the manuscript of *The Storm,* including his own typewritten introduction. Norm La Coe himself lived in Micanopy and would probably have known Mr. Briskey. Gary Nippes managed Briskey's bookstore for fifteen years until Mr. Briskey died in January 2014, and Nippes continued to operate the store until it closed a few months later. Mr. Nippes and his wife donated the manuscript to the University of Florida in September 2015. It seems likely that the manuscript had remained in Briskey's vast inventory of Florida literature, memorabilia, and so on until Mr. and Mrs. Nippes made their donation.[11]

The Copyist and the Illustrator

At the conclusion to his introduction, Norm La Coe speculates that "the manuscript [of] *The Storm* probably was copied by a professional penman for submission to a publisher" because, as he correctly asserts, the handwriting does not match Corinna's or Ellen's (33). Still, since a person's handwriting can be affected by numerous factors and change significantly over the years, it might not always provide a reliable indication of authorship, so the possibility remains that Ellen or Corinna penned the manuscript of *The Storm*. The handwriting nonetheless does cast serious doubt on either sister's having written out the manuscript, so Mr. La Coe's suggestion that Ellen must have had someone else copy it is most likely correct. Another fact to consider is that Ellen's eyesight became increasingly poor during her years in New York, which often prevented her from physically writing herself. Between 1850 and her death in 1862, Ellen lived with her children in various places in New York, was in contact with people in the publishing business, and of course could have found a copyist, yet hiring a copyist probably would have been an expense beyond her limited means. Nevertheless, her vision problems and tight budget did not halt her literary efforts: she reveals in a May 16, 1860, letter that her oldest daughter, Georgia, sixteen years old at the time and a good student, was serving as her amanuensis—a fact that explains how the manuscript could be her story, or hers and Corinna's, but not in her or Corinna's hand.[12] The manuscript appears to have been written in Spencerian script, a style of handwriting invented in the 1840s and in widespread use in American schools by 1850—too late for Corinna's and Ellen's school days, but just in time for Georgia to have learned it in school.[13] The Anderson-Brown collection holds several of Georgia Anderson's letters: one written to her brother, Edward "Will" Anderson, at West Point on November 11, 1860, is perhaps the best-preserved example. A comparison of this letter and the manuscript of *The Storm* demonstrates that the two hands are similar though not precisely identical. The person copying *The Storm* certainly wrote as carefully as possible with the best quality of pen and paper available, while Georgia no doubt wrote her letters in comparative haste with whatever supplies she had, including an obviously leaky pen for this particular letter. If Georgia indeed wrote out or copied *The Storm* for her mother, there is no reason to expect the manuscript's calligraphy to be an exact match for the handwriting in her letters.

Given that the story's author was almost definitely a woman with extensive firsthand knowledge of Key West, which at this time had a population of less than three thousand, and that the author lived there sometime after the 1846 hurricane and later had access to *The Potiphar Papers* published in 1853 in New York, there would be very few, if any, other candidates as likely to be the author of *The Storm* as Ellen Brown Anderson. The case for her authorship rises to the level of confident attribution as defined by Harold Love: "[A] confident attribution might rest on one particular result... with generally supportive internal and external evidence and with no tenable alternative" (226). In the case of this story, the "one particular result" is the long-term storage of the manuscript with the Anderson-Brown family's personal correspondence in the Washington, D.C., family home and the documented evidence that John Traynor Jr. took the manuscript to Gainesville in 1972 along with family letters related to Florida. The external evidence includes factors such as the sisters' residence in Key West at the approximate time of the story's setting; internal evidence includes elements such as the similarity of the descriptions and ideas in the story to those in the Brown sisters' letters, especially Ellen's. Evidence that favors attributing the story's authorship to Ellen rather than Corinna includes the reference to Mrs. Potiphar and Ellen's determined pursuit of writing as a career at the time when *The Storm* most likely was composed; at this same time, Corinna's serious health issues cast doubt on her ability to contribute to the story. Currently, there is "no tenable alternative" to this attribution.[14]

Therefore, the most reasonable solution to the mystery of the authorship of the manuscript is that between 1850 and 1862, Ellen Brown Anderson, perhaps with early assistance from Corinna Brown Aldrich, wrote *The Storm*.

Also included with the manuscript donated to The P. K. Yonge Library are three pen-and-ink illustrations specifically designed for scenes in *The Storm*. They are certainly the work of a trained artist or artists, but the faint remainder of penciled vanishing point lines suggests that they were done quickly, perhaps as samples for Ellen to consider. The first of these, which is placed immediately after page twenty-three of the manuscript, pictures Jenny Greenough with a book in her lap, seated at a tea table in a well-furnished room, protected by her large, tent-like mosquito net. This illustration is signed, but the signature is mostly indecipherable except for the final initial, which appears to be a "B." The other illustrations appear together after page sixty-three. The second illustration depicts the moonlight-flooded view from the entrance to the Greenoughs' Key West house, and the third shows Jenny floating on an object from the wreckage of the steamer she was taking to New York. These last two illustrations are unsigned but closely resemble the first in style (see figures 12, 13, and 14). It seems unlikely that Ellen could have afforded to hire an artist for this job, but fortunately, her brother Mannevillette was an accomplished professional artist who would have handled the job free of charge. At about the time when the sisters moved to Key West, Mannevillette returned to the United States from an extended stay in Europe studying art. He took up residence in Utica, New York, where he lived until his death in 1896, so he was in close contact with Ellen when she and Corinna moved to New York City.

Nevertheless, despite the similarity in style of the three illustrations, it is not certain that the same artist did all three. If Mannevillette completed only the signed illustration, then it seems quite possible that Ellen's younger daughter, Villette, could have prepared the other two illustrations for the story while Ellen was living or even after her death in 1862. No verifiable examples of Villette's artwork are available, but family letters reveal that Mannevillette gave both of Ellen's girls art lessons, so for Villette's style to be similar to Mannevillette's would be natural. That Villette secured a job in the Washington, D.C., patent office drafting inventions and that she gave drawing lessons on the side provide evidence of her artistic skill. With Mannevillette making all three illustrations, or Mannevillette doing the first and Villette or even Georgia doing the others, the illustrations would have added no expense to the project. Elizabeth Traynor, Ellen's great-

great-great-great-niece, herself a professional illustrator, believes that it is more likely that Ellen's daughters did the illustrations since the work is not quite up to Mannevillette's standards. I defer to her professional artistic judgment, but the initial "B" on the first illustration would only be appropriate for Mannevillette Brown and not for Georgia or Villette Anderson, and the quality of the work might have been less than his very best for a sample composed quickly for his sister to consider.

Notes

1. To guide my analysis of all available evidence relating to the authorship of the text, I have consulted Harold Love's *Attributing Authorship: An Introduction*. Love categorizes the kinds of evidence generally used to establish authorship of a disputed or unattributed text:

   > Attribution studies distinguish conventionally between internal and external evidence. Broadly, internal evidence is that from the work itself and external evidence that from the social world within which the work is created, promulgated and read; but there will always be overlap. Often one kind of evidence only acquires meaning by reference to the other.... External evidence ... covers the following kinds: (1) Contemporary attributions ... from documents purporting to impart information about the circumstances of composition—especially diaries, correspondence, publishers' records, and records of legal proceedings; (2) Biographical evidence, which would include information about a putative author's allegiances, whereabouts, dates, personal ties, and political and religious affiliations; (3) The history of earlier attributions of the work.... Internal evidence ... covers (1) Stylistic evidence; (2) Self-reference and self-presentation within the work; (3) Evidence from the themes, ideas, beliefs and conceptions of genre manifested in the work. (51)

   Love adds that "The second class of external evidence and the third of internal will inevitably overlap" (51); my own argument primarily rests on evidence from these two categories.

2. See Catherine Gallagher, *Nobody's Story: The Vanishing Acts of Women Writers in the Marketplace, 1670–1920*.

3. For instance, in a letter in which Corinna reveals to Mannevillette that Ellen's "Novel in a Nut-Shell" would be published in the September 1850 issue of the *Knickerbocker*, Corinna tells him to destroy the letter and not reveal to anyone who wrote the story.

4. County attorney by profession, Mr. La Coe (1932–2022) had an extensive background in Alachua County history: he helped establish the Alachua County Historical Society, drafted the ordinance to create the Alachua County Historical Commission, and helped found the Micanopy Historical Society.

5. John Traynor Jr. (1939–2003) was married to Elizabeth "Betsy" Traynor, the great-great-great-niece of Ellen Brown Anderson. When Mannevillette Sullivan, another great-great-niece of Ellen Anderson, purchased these letters (or in some cases, copies of them) from Mr. Goolsby and other sources, she combined them with letters that were still held by family members. She then donated them to the United States Military Academy in 1985 as "The Anderson-Brown Papers," which designation I will use when referring to the entire collection of around nine hundred nineteenth-century family letters and other manuscripts. I will refer to the portion of this collection that Mr. Traynor took to Gainesville as "The Traynor collection."

6. Mannevillette Sullivan.

7. The first of these, dated May 1, 1972, is from Mr. La Coe to Mr. John J. Traynor Jr. In it, Mr. La Coe responds to a letter from Mr. Traynor sent on April 24, 1972, and expresses strong interest in examining "The John J. Traynor, Jr. Collection" or copies of the contents due to their historical value. In a letter of October 12, 1972, La Coe tells Traynor that "Dr. Charles Hoffman has gone to Arizona to teach. He left the letters in my care and custody." Photocopies of the Traynor collection were also held at the University of Florida, as confirmed in a May 8, 1972, letter to John Traynor from Elizabeth Alexander, librarian at The P. K. Yonge Library of Florida History. She thanks him for allowing the staff to "xerox the John J. Traynor, Jr. Collection. Mr. Norm La Coe has graciously supplied this collection to us. These valuable items will be catalogued and made available to use by Florida historians and scholars."

8. Jane Meyer Gill, Ellen Brown Anderson's great-great-great-niece; her husband, Raymond Gill; the late Betsy Meyer Traynor (mentioned above); and Elizabeth Traynor, John and Besty's daughter, have graciously shared their family history with me in person and by email.

9. Elizabeth Traynor adds that Mary Gedney Meyer, Elizabeth's grandmother and one of only two surviving grandchildren of Will Anderson, gave John direct permission to sell the contents of the collection or "do whatever you like with them." In an email sent to me on May 6, 2018, Raymond Gill remarked, "I remember Mary Meyer, Jane's mother, telling me that her great-grandmother wrote a novel." Mary Meyer, who was George Anderson's niece, like other family members, had seen the collection of family papers many times. The novel she referred to was almost definitely *The Storm*, since there was no other story nearly that long in the collection, but she never explained to Mr. Gill why she believed Ellen wrote it, and not Corinna.

10. Mr. La Coe attempted to find out more about *The Storm* by writing to the Monroe County Public Library in Key West on July 12, 1973. On July 19, he received a reply from Betty Bruce, who identified herself as "the Researcher for our Library's Florida Collection." She explained, "The letters and the manuscripts you describe sound very interesting, and I feel sure they would be useful in our research on Key West history. I hope that it will be possible for us to obtain them for our collection. . . . As to the manuscript, I, of course, can only say that we would have to read it and try to discover if it had been published. . . . We are most interested in hearing further about this material so please let us hear from you or the owner of the letters and manuscript."

11 For more about O. J. Briskey's bookstore and its Florida-related material, see Emily Miller's "Micanopy Loses an Icon in Bookseller O. J. Briskey" and Laura E. Ide's "Bookseller O. J. Briskey Still Missed in Micanopy."
12 Anderson-Brown Papers.
13 See H. C. Spencer's *Spencerian Key to Practical Penmanship*. For a quick look at the history of Spencerian handwriting instruction and some samples from an instruction book published in 1866, see Jeffrey Makala's "The Spencerian and Palmer Methods."
14 No other possible author has been proposed by audience members from two conference papers that I have delivered on the story, by readers of my two published articles on *The Storm*, or by listeners to Christopher Nank's interview with me on "The Florida Book Club" podcast.

APPENDIX A

Ellen Brown Anderson's "A Novel in a Nut-Shell"

On September 12, 1850, Corinna wrote to Mannevillette to reveal that Ellen had published a story, "A Novel in a Nut-Shell," in the *Knickerbocker*. As far as I have been able to determine, this is Ellen's only story published in her lifetime. The story is unsigned, but Corinna identifies Ellen as the author and tells Mannevillette to pick up the forthcoming September 1850 issue of the magazine, where he would find the story. The magazine's table of contents identifies the author as The Condensationalist, a pseudonym that Ellen also used for "Thoughts on the Influence of Novels," an unpublished essay now in her descendants' possession. Although publishing the story was a happy event, the sisters' failure to receive fair compensation for their work continued. Corinna explains that for this story, "we received only the poor broth of the compliment of publishing; for this reason, I refused to let them have my article, *it being much longer and of course more valuable.*—He said, afterwards, when he found I would not give it to him, that he would give me *something* for it. Perhaps, I may let him have it. But, I repeat, don't speak of it, and tear up this letter and burn it in your old stove" (Anderson-Brown Papers, 9–12–1850). Sadly, many other nineteenth-century authors suffered similar treatment from publishers. According to Jonathan Wells, "Publishers often took advantage of their authors" (81).

Set in Portsmouth, New Hampshire, and Boston, Massachusetts, the tale follows the fortunes of Louisa Goldensoul, a bright, talented, good-hearted, but poor washerwoman's daughter who struggles to improve life for her family. Told from the narrative perspective of Fred Clacket, the man who falls in love with Louisa and marries her despite her family's low standing, the tale shows Louisa's talent, hard work, and virtue leading to eventual prosperity and happiness. The story has realistic description, individualized characters, a moralizing narrative, and some original verse. Published at about the time that Ellen would probably have been working on, or at least planning, *The Storm*, the basic plot and style of "A Novel in a Nut-Shell" resemble certain aspects of *The Storm*: the protagonist is a young woman of good character who, at the story's ending, marries a good man who recognizes her worth and rewards her with prosperity, which he earns by hard work. Like *The Storm*, this story displays Ellen's concern with education, as seen here: "Happily and wisely is it ordered by Providence that the general tendency of learning is to improve the heart and liberalize the understanding; and to their praise be it spoken, those who have the charge of schools generally attend to the moral training of those they educate" ("Novel" 217). Resembling the style and tone of *The Storm*, this story has long passages of moralizing narrative digression, as in this paragraph:

> Seldom indeed does our fate turn upon the hinges we mould for it. Accident juts in, on every side, and jostles us from the paths we have carefully laid out. Yet although scarcely ever in the way designed, naught is seriously undertaken and eagerly pursued but leads to results curious, astonishing, or it may be ridiculous, even as is the ability and ardor which undertakes. But for apparent accident, what might have been the fate of Bonaparte? What of Europe? What of the world? The shot which pierced the coat of WASHINGTON *might have* ruined America. In all things a WISE HAND directs, which we too rarely think of. None can foretell the end of any beginning, howsoever wisely planned; none but that EYE which seeth not as man seeth; that POWER which has promised repeated blessings on those who trust in it: which is strength to the poor, a refuge from the storm, and a shadow from the heat. Whoso putteth his trust in the LORD, mercy embraceth him on every side. Louisa thought of the overruling DEITY, and trusted. ("Novel" 224)

See the passage on Christian faith on pages 63 and 64 of *The Storm* for similar narrative commentary.

A NOVEL IN A NUT-SHELL

> Is she gentle—apt to please?
> Witty, pretty, less or more?
> P'shaw! what foolish questions these!
> Is she rich, or is she poor?

In the days of my boyhood, when I was a sophomore of C——college, I once had occasion to travel through P——, a large New-England town, on my route to my *alma mater*, and we passed the large schoolhouse just as the girls came pouring forth, at the close of the afternoon lessons. The stage stopped at a hotel near, and I, with one or two others of about my own appearance and calibre, strolled up the street to take a look at them. Boys are not always very gentlemanly, nor girls ladylike; and in this instance the bounds of good manners were certainly overstepped. There was one young lady who attracted my attention as being particularly pretty, and in an effort to be smart in her hearing, I said to my companions: "Behold the future mothers of the land!"

"The future statesmen and orators!" immediately rejoined one of the girls. "Lou., do you hear those impudent fellows?"

"Yes," replied Miss Lou., who was the one to whom I had taken a fancy; and turning her head, she said with great archness:

> "The green young saplings which we see,
> Advancing, grow to trees;
> Behold! how rich the land must be
> To bear such sprouts as these!"

Whereupon they all laughed merrily, and then ran away. We had paused to hear her speech, but they gave us no chance to answer; so we returned to the hotel, feeling very much as if we had the worst of it, but that graceful form, that comical expression, and above all that bright face, haunted me for weeks after I returned to my studies, and were the beau ideal of many a sonnet and improvised romance. In truth, I never forgot her: and circumstances in after years brought to my knowledge the whole history of her who was my boyhood's dream. This was so unlike the history of heroines in general, that I have thought it worthy of being written, in the hope that the events of our lives may benefit others, if any there be who can profit by their neighbors' experience. Indeed I sometimes think that the heroes and heroines of novels and tales have as many, if not more, practical followers than the sages and apostles of wisdom.

Thus, while I went on my way, musing on my unknown beauty, fancying her in all manner of romantic situations—in carriages, on horseback, by the side of precipices, in splendid drawing-rooms, in hair-breadth escapes, beset with unfit suitors, or teazed by stingy or tyrannical (and always rich) relations, for there is no manner of situation in life except the right one in which I did not place her—behold! she went on her way to her home. This was in one of the most obscure streets of the town, in a very mean, unpainted, little, one-story house. Here she seated herself upon an old frame of a chair, with a piece of skin tied in it for a bottom. She laid the slate and two or three books she had carried in her arms on the floor beside her, and commenced chatting to a fat, old, hard-working character who was there, diligently making tea and johnny-cake for supper.

"Mother," said the girl, "as we came from school we saw the stage passengers getting out, and among them were some of the boys going to college. We said something about them which I think the fellows overheard, for they turned round and looked after us."

"I'll warrant you made a grammet at them," said the mother; but the girl continued, without heeding:

"I wish Tom could go to college."

"Tom go to college!" exclaimed the old woman, laughing at the idea.

"Yes, why not? Tom is as smart a boy as any in his school:

> A man a locomotive is.
> Steam raising every hour;
> And Tom within that head of his
> Has got a twelve-horse power.

Sometimes I think that if I could get something to do, maybe we both together could send him. I should so love to see Tom a gentleman!"

"P'shaw, gal! your wits are turned, through going to school. If I can get Tom 'prenticed to a good trade, as his father was before him, he'll be gentleman enough for me. But I should like to hear how you would set about getting the money.["]

"Why, you know, Aunt Louisa keeps a boarding-house in B——. Well now, mother, if you would give me all the money I could make on Wednesday and Saturday afternoons, and mornings and evenings, and other odd times, by helping you, I think I could get enough to go and make her a visit. You know I am named after her: perhaps she would put me in the way of doing something. B——is a large place." Here Louisa paused a moment. In truth, she had no very definite idea of what she wished her aunt to do for her; but she desired greatly to make her a visit. Her hope by day and her dream by night was, by some means or other, to obtain for herself and her brother a station in that rank of life from which poverty now debarred them. Once at her aunt's house, she would have one step taken on the ladder of her ambition. Great projects are never born full-grown. Like every earthly thing, they have their infancy, their childhood, their youth, and their maturity, and death arrests them at any stage. Meantime, to divert her mother from a more close inquiry until her plans should be fully ripe she related a number of histories she had read of men who had become distinguished, from the humblest situations in life, until the old woman was quite bewildered with what had been told her; for she was profoundly ignorant, not being able even to read. Yet she was one who had been cast in nature's noblest mould; or, to speak after Doctor Johnson's celebrated simile, she was a most beautiful and available block of marble, which had lain unsought and unfound in the wide wilderness of poverty. But HE who knoweth the hiding-place of every jewel had not created her nor her great soul in vain, although but the widow of a poor mechanic, and reduced to maintain herself and her two children by taking in washing and ironing. Strong, healthy, and cheerful by nature, accustomed always to spend what she earned, and as she earned it, she had no idea of saving money, nor any ability to calculate the amount she could save. Not so Louisa; she could count, and she could calculate.

Ignorant people have very little notion of the virtue of education: but Mrs. Goldensoul loved her children; they were her pets. When little, it had been a pleasure rather than a task to her strong nerves and hardened muscles to wash and dress them neat and clean; and when so washed and dressed, she behooved to have some object for which to do it. School! that was where other people's children went, and it appeared a very fit place to send them to display their pretty frocks and faces; and then they looked so sweet, walking off together, that it was a sufficient inducement to send them just to see them go. In process of time the children began to have their little school ambitions and cares. Their mother was their confidant, and they were her companions. She rejoiced in their successes and sympathized with their troubles; until, from the ascendancy which knowledge is sure to gain over ignorance, she came to look upon their acquirements as miraculous, and to be almost entirely influenced by their opinions. Not above her business herself, she had not taught her children to be so; and Louisa, as she assisted at the ironing-table and related to her mother the wonders of history and science, made a most agreeable associate; and what marvel if she became at length the master-spirit? Had she professed to have obtained the secret of alchemy, or to have found Aladdin's lamp (which, by the way, I think she had; but that will appear), her mother would have believed her undoubtingly. Happily and wisely is it ordered by Providence that the general tendency of learning is to improve the heart and liberalize the understanding; and to their praise be it spoken, those who have the charge of schools generally attend to the moral training of those they educate. But neither had the mother omitted to send her children to the Sunday school; and, by so doing, had unwittingly provided another antidote to the dangers of her own ignorance and blind affection.

With this insight into their circumstances, it is not surprising that Louisa obtained her mother's consent to her proposition, and what was more important, succeeded in inspiring her with some sort of faith in it; albeit the mother's hope looked not beyond a situation as school-teacher or milliner's apprentice. Far otherwise the daughter. When has ever youth set bounds to its imaginings, or ardent fancy chained itself to slow-moving reason? Her head was now quite filled with this half-formed scheme. She was a conqueror, in her way, as great as many whom poets have sung and historians lauded; for she laid plans and overcame difficulties. Hers was no visionary head to dream for idle hands. Eminently practical was she in all her views; at least so would her biographer have written, had she been one of the before-mentioned heroes. With diligent hands, with industry early and late, at an exercise far from unhealthy, and with a mind buoyed up by hope, *she exerted her talent*; and her health, instead of suffering, was even improved thereby. It cost her some qualms of school-acquired pride as she went with the little brother for whom she was to do such great things to fetch and carry the enormous bundles of clothes; but, "No matter, Tom," said she:

> "Alladan rubbed a magic lamp for wealth and great renown,
> And we with these old clothes must tramp
> To bring our castle down.

> "He did but rub the lamp, and brought
> A genius to his side;
> And I shall rub the clothes for naught
> But rank and wealth allied.

> "For what is magic but the ways
> Of knowledge, work and care?
> It needs but have these three to raise a genius any where."

Tom expressed sufficient approbation of the rhymes; and Louisa, having, as usual when annoyed, got rid of her trouble by measuring it out, hugged her project to her heart, and exercise kept her from dyspepsia.

Time sped; the little pile of money soon increased, and the moderate sum required was at last told over. The doting mother hated to part with her darling, and Tom wished that he could go also; but the minds of all three were so completely imbued with the hope of prosperity, that no objection was made; and Louisa, with her small means and great anticipations, went on her way to the city, where no one would recognise her as the washerwoman's daughter.

Aunt Louisa Moskey, as hinted above, kept a boarding-house; one of those numberless establishments which abound in large cities, where economy is the means and end, the plan and result, of every department, and where dwell persons desirous of economizing; poverty and avarice associating and consoling each other. Here were the medical student and the merchant's clerk, the poor lawyer and the rich bankrupt, the independent young lady, whose age is among forgotten things, and the meddlesome old woman, whose husband is in the same category; for prices, victuals and accommodations were each under the fashionable standard. And here Louisa arrived, in the middle of summer. At that time the boarding-houses in B——do not overflow with customers, and she was received with some charity, inasmuch as she did not come at an inconvenient season.

The aunt was a thin, care-worn looking body, with two or three children, and a great many anxieties. Oh, the devotees of mammon! how hard they work! how bitterly they fare! Her ignorance of the world, and the sense of her own daring, gave Louisa a feeling of uneasiness, which this lady's manner was not calculated, entirely to remove; nevertheless, with the help of a very acute understanding, she contrived to be somewhat at home. Tea was ready, soon after her arrival. Seated for the first time, in the company of those she considered her superiors at least in the knowledge of etiquette, she was silent and observing; being far too good a general, to parade her ignorance by pretending to manners she only guessed at.

After tea she went not into the parlor, she glanced at that in passing; but into her aunt's private room. This was not cunning; but a sort of sense of right. She had come to visit her aunt, and she wanted her favor. To win it, she began with an indefinite intention of doing her a kindness; or in other words, a simple wish to make herself useful. In her aunt's room, she found the children. There was a boy somewhat younger than herself, puzzling over a lesson; two very cross little girls teasing him; and a pile of sheets and pillow cases to be made. She sat down in a rocking chair; took the youngest child in her arms, and played with it, and sang to it, and very soon attracted the attention of the elder girl; and the boy was left to pursue his studies unmolested. So that in a short time she had at least made peace where there was usually war. The youngest child fell asleep; she laid it on a lounge, and the second one claimed its place. By this time Mrs. Moskey came in with a servant to put the children to bed; and she expressed her gratification at finding them so quiet. Louisa parted with her other cousin; and seeing her aunt commence sewing on the sheets, she volunteered her assistance there, which was readily accepted. Mrs. M. declaring "she was in a prodigious hurry to get them done, as she had a great deal to do, which she wished to accomplish before the house should be again crowded with boarders. She had hired Mrs. Slowman at two dollars a week, but it appeared to her she would never finish anything." So Louisa passed the remainder of the evening in helping to bring up the arrears of Mrs. Slowman; and in listening to the tune of her aunt's troubles; which latter consisted in running the scale up and down: from the lowest to the highest note through every pitch and tone and variation of domestic grievances in the shape of servants. She really felt a sympathy for her aunt, and a desire to relieve some of these sad trials.

The next morning she was up early as was her wont; and if nothing else had influenced her, ennui, at the loss of her usual occupations would have caused her to wish for employment. Persons of good health and strong minds are seldom disposed to idleness; and when to these are added the habit of industry, the former becomes a punishment. She followed her aunt around with cheerful smiles, ready wit and helping hands. With perfect sincerity she praised the breakfast. Boarding-house keepers are particularly vulnerable on the score of their tables and housekeeping; and although this was doubtless gross flattery in fact; yet indeed the table stood fair in comparison with the washer-woman's; and it was received in good faith, because Mrs. M. persuaded herself to believe it, and desired that others should do the same. Thus did Louisa acquire good opinions; and thus she went on. She assisted at making the pies; she lent a hand at the desserts; she helped to nurse the children, manufacture the clothes, and renovate the finery. Not that she was an adept at all these things, far from it; but she learned from occasion; and with her good heart and fine natural abilities, she began to take such an interest in the assistance she gave, that she was in some danger of forgetting her principal object.

Meantime Aunt Moskey was not unmindful of the value of her visitor. Selfishness always renders people shortsighted; and she began to study how she should retain her; she thought of offering her wages. Feeling rich in unpaid-for services, she hauled out her old garments for new uses; and from among the surplus, she gave Louisa a white muslin, which had been a very pretty dress; and which, in new hands, became one again; a yard or two of blue ribbon, and these things were received with such girlish delight, that she added to them some other finery.

All persons are delighted with gratitude, there is no more certain indication of a noble nature, than the ability to receive a small favor gracefully.

It is true the gifts were very trifling; especially when compared with the services rendered and the obligation incurred. But Mrs. Moskey was poor; at least she thought herself so, although well established in a good and lucrative calling. I call it lucrative; it is true a fortune would not accrue from it in a very short time; but to one boarder who cheated her, she had ten who paid well; and I think if it were essential to this story, I could show that if she had husbanded her resources properly, and rated her necessities reasonably, she would have made a very comfortable living. But her habit of mind was to set herself in comparison with every person above her in the scale of wealth, self-indulgence, and worldly distinction; and "forgetting those things which were behind, to press toward the mark of the high calling" of earthly greatness. Beside she was bilious, and that made her indolent and irritable, selfish, and would-be fashionable; here was an ocean of wants to which the income of a paltry boarding-house, was not a bucketful. I do not wonder she thought herself poor. But although it is true that I have not painted Mrs. Moskey very loveable, still, there are much worse people than her in the world. There are those who would have thought the utmost a poor girl in Louisa's situation could have done, would not have entitled her to their good graces. She felt mean at the gifts she offered; but their value was so magnified by the skill exercised in making use of them, that she was restored by it to her own good opinion. It never occurred to her that one principal cause of Louisa's gratitude was the friendly feeling which the gifts evinced. There are those who value a present only for its intrinsic worth: these are hard to satisfy; and there are those who take largely into account the feeling which prompts the giver. Oh! what a world of difference lies between these considerations! It is not in the nature of feeling to stand still, whether for good or evil; and Mrs. Moskey began to plan other favors for her niece, which should not cost her an outlay of money. She had the usual knowledge of the prevailing fashion possessed by a dweller in a large city; and Louisa was neither blind nor stupid. So under their combined efforts the white muslin, the blue ribbon, and Louisa, were converted into quite a distinguished-looking young lady. The latter was pretty, healthy and cheerful; she had a good figure, a good heart, good sense and a good education: these were her advantages. Boarding-house keepers are, from the nature of their occupation, very apt to be match-makers; opportunity continually furnishing them with temptation; and the aunt began to study what old characters of her acquaintance, having money, could be tempted by these goods, against the odds of low-born poverty, to marry her niece. The eldest of the two little girls was taking her first lessons on the piano; and Louisa, from sitting by her and taking notice, soon began to acquire an insight into the science of music; and often would pass a twilight or an hour when the parlor was otherwise deserted, putting in practice her picked-up knowledge.

CHAPTER SECOND

I HAD finished my collegiate course, and was about to commence the study of the law under a celebrated counsellor at Boston, and for a comfortable (I believe the word means cheap—I know fashionable means dear) boarding-house had been recommended to Mrs. Moskey's. Behold me, green and aspiring, sent into the parlor to await the mistress of the house. The piano suddenly stopped as I entered, and a young woman arose from it hastily, and in charming confusion, and my lost Pleiad stood before me. It was but for an instant, for she left the room immediately. I made no difficulty of my terms with Mrs. M. I could not tell whether I had consented to occupy the garret or the cellar, much less the price. I was ambitious; I had my way to make in the world. What knowledge I had will be seen by the use I made of it. My head now became entirely filled with this girl. The white dress and blue ribbon did their full amount of work with me. I took my seat beside her, whenever and wherever she appeared. I walked with her; I talked with her. She was very intelligent, and had a great deal of harmless drollery, which rendered her exceedingly fascinating. She who had nothing to boast of in family or fortune, and was too conscientious to lie, was consequently never egotistical. Her hands, although by no means bad-looking, she was conscious had seen hard work, and she never displayed them; either smoothing down the sides of her hair, or playing with her mouth, or in, as it were habitually, running over the keys of Imagination's piano. What wonder I thought her a high bred lady. How often have I admired the simplicity of her dress; its freedom from tinsel and ornament, which taste indeed had arranged, but I guessed not that poverty had prescribed. I had no distinct intention of marrying immediately; but I was daily getting more and more in love, and I did not conceal it. Indeed, my jealousy broke over all bounds if she appeared to take pleasure in the society of any other person than myself.

This state of things did not at all please Mrs. Moskey. It deranged her plans entirely.

"The family is very respectable, and he is as proud as Lucifer," she would say. "Beside, he is so handsome and so talented," (so she was pleased to say of me,) "he could marry any girl in B. He would not look at you if he knew your mother worked for her living. If ever Fred. Clacket marries, he will marry for money."

Louisa nearly choked when these and like inuer does were thrown out. At last one evening her aunt took her into her room purposely to lay the case in all its bearings before her. After a proper exordium, she continued:

"There is old Captain Smalet would marry you in a moment. There is Quandary; what if he is dowdy? He says you are just the girl he would like to have. And there is Riquets; he drives his carriage and has a beautiful country-seat. Don't spoil your chance in this way."

"The old curmudgeons!" exclaimed Louisa. "I would not marry one of them if I could combine the advantages of all. Who would care to ride in a carriage, if they must have old Riquets always beside them? They say he was a tailor, and a good one too, both for cut and price:

> "THAT talent answers various ends, is proved at any rate,
> The tailor who can make a man can make a vast estate."

["]As for Smalet, his first wife had to carry the bellows to bed to inflate his lungs whenever he had an attack of asthma, for fear the dear old soul might die before the doctor could get to him. No, no, aunt! if I work that hard it shall be for something to gratify my eyes at least:

> "WHEN I assume a matron's cares for such old daddy's healths,
> The wealth must borrow cupid's wings, and Cupid fly on Wealth's."

"Rhyme is not reason," interrupted Mrs. Moskey.

"Don't you like that?" said Louisa, "well that is not very good. I'll try again." But though she spoke banteringly, she sighed bitterly: "Ah me":

> "SINCE wealth has wings, and love as well,
> And even both may fly,
> And taste is apt to stay a spell,
> I'll try and please my eye."

"Why child you are crazy, to go on as you do!" again broke in her aunt. "You are ruining yourself, and all I have done for you is thrown away."

And here she became so zealous, that she began to threaten; darkly and distantly indeed, just to infuse a slight suspicion into Louisa's mind, that if she did not conduct herself more circumspectly with regard to her lover, she would blow her sky-high in his estimation by telling him her whole history. To these insinuations Louisa replied humorously: "Aunt, I'll tell you what["]:

"I'D rather wash a hundred years to earn a single groat,
Than blow the bellows once a week down Daddy Small-clothes' throat."

["]Good night!" It was late, and she went to her own room, weary, disgusted and wretched.

What a change was wrought in her! What was station to her now, if it could not be enjoyed with him she loved? She sat down and reflected on what had been said to her. Neither was it the first time she had so reflected; but such thoughts were painful, and first love is a bright intoxication, an infatuation, a madness! Now, conscience bade her look her own conduct in the face. Was she not tacitly deceiving her lover? And then her mother and her brother came before her, and fancy painted all that money could do for them; but there arose the heart-sickening prospect of marrying——! "Bah! Have I not hands? Do I not know how? Is there not work enough to be done? My mother! my brother! there is nothing in this world for me, but I am for you. Oh! how gladly, how eagerly will I work; but not for you, no, not even for you, will I make myself a legal mistress. Not for you, will I insult the holy altar, standing before it to vow a lie; to promise to love and honor where no love, no honor can exist. No! no! no!"

The last words were uttered aloud and resolutely; and as she uttered them, she arose from the statue-like position in which she had been sitting. Determination gave relief to her feelings, and she went to bed, but not to sleep. There was no sleep for her; she could not rest. Thought was torture. Starting up with strong and sudden resolution, she seized her trunk, gathered together her clothes, packed them into it, and dressed herself for travelling. Then taking her lamp, she returned to her aunt's room. That room, which she had left so short a time before, was now silent, save from the deep breathing of the sleeper. Yes, she could sleep. She had filled the heart of another with remorse and bitter anxiety; she had bereft it of the power of rest or peace; and this purely and avowedly for worldly reasons, and then laid down to sleep, saying: "I have done my duty." Oh, human beings! who among us, know their duty? This woman really believed she was studying her niece's best interests.

Louisa sat down at her aunt's writing desk and wrote the following note:

"MY FRIEND: Imperious duty calls me suddenly to return to my beloved home. As the cars will leave very early this morning, I shall not see you again, and I cannot resist the temptation of saying 'Good-by!' Yours, Louisa."

She closed and directed it, saying to herself: ["]I ought not to do this but——I cannot help it."

With some trepidation she went and placed it in the glass where invitations were usually left, then returning to her aunt's room, she awoke her. The latter was greatly surprised; but Louisa stopped her exclamations, saying: "My dear aunt, I have thought all night of what you have said: my resolution is taken. It is useless to talk to me: I want to see my mother. Shall not one of the servants go down with me to the cars?"

Poor Mrs. Moskey! She had some distant notion of what was right; she flounced out of bed, and was in great anxiety to do something. She begged Louisa to write to her, and picked up some presents for her sister and nephew; and as she thought of what a loss she was about to sustain, she asked her to promise to return. Louisa thanked her, kissed her, and left her to go and bid the children good-by; and then departed from that city, from which she had anticipated so much and realized so little.

Oh, dreamer! where are all your bright hopes now? How is the air-built castle vanished! She drops a burning tear over the few and trifling presents which are all she brings in its stead.

Seldom indeed does our fate turn upon the hinges we mould for it. Accident juts in, on every side, and jostles us from the paths we have carefully laid out. Yet although scarcely ever in the way designed, naught is seriously undertaken and eagerly pursued but leads to results curious, astonishing, or it may be ridiculous, even as is the ability and ardor which undertakes. But for apparent accident, what might have been the fate of Bonaparte? What of Europe? What of the world? The shot which pierced the coat of WASHINGTON *might have* ruined America. In all things, a Wise HAND directs, which we too rarely think of. None can fortell the end of any beginning, howsoever wisely planned; none but that EYE which seeth not as man seeth; that POWER which has promised repeated blessings on those who trust in it: which is strength to the poor, a refuge from the storm, and a shadow from the heat. Whoso putteth his trust in the LORD, mercy embraceth him on every side. Louisa thought of the overruling DEITY, and trusted.

She arrived at her home. Her mother was in ecstasies of delight at seeing her darling once again. The child's fancies had faded from her mind so soon as the genius which kept them bright had departed; and the poor old woman had only moped and mourned at her absence. The little brother had missed his companion, and sighed for her return. There was nothing but joy to greet her. No disappointment weighed on their spirits. No sad recollections clouded the past; no dismal forebodings darkened the future. For them there was but hope fulfilled, their loved one safe at home. Oh, how bright smiles can make cheerful the humblest abode! It is not in elevated rank, it is not in splendid furniture; it is not in costly carriages nor magnificent buildings that happiness dwells; it is in innocent and loving hearts, wherever they abide. Still Louisa felt as if she had somehow cheated them. Often in wandering about the great city she had ached at her heart's core for the means of gratifying one single wish: to bring home to her mother and brother a portion of the new and beautiful things she saw every where displayed. The presents her aunt and the children had given her, with the purchases made with all her money, she had carefully hoarded. Yet they seemed such a mere nothing in comparison with what she would have done, had she had the means, that she feared to offer them. But they who had fostered no expectations were made quite rich, and thought she had accomplished quite enough by her journey. So much are opinions the effect of imagination.

She had worked before for hope; she set to work now to drive away the remembrance of it. She worked harder than before; but her mother lamented that she was not so cheerful. She strove to overcome this. There was a world of agony within her breast; there was a world, also, of resolution. Your self-afflicted dreamers, your mourners over imaginary woes, may afford to be idle, and contemplate their miseries; but action is the antidote to real heart-ache; and as disease instinctively seeks its cure, so will the heart, smarting under real torture, seek relief in employment; in employment as constant as the pain it would forget; in employment as fatiguing as the pain it would wear out.

Louisa kept her promise, and wrote to her aunt; and with longing curiosity awaited an answer. A letter came, but not from Mrs. Moskey: it was from her lover. It was a passionate ebullition of love and pique; of love, full, warm and confiding, which kept no bounds of discretion, and pique at fancied slight. "Surely there was no part of my conduct that could have made you doubt the sincerity of my affection for you," said this wise letter; "and if I did not directly offer to you, as your aunt seems to intimate, was it kind or candid to leave me thus? You knew I could not follow you, talk as they will of love's laughing at impossibilities. I cannot help fancying that some regard for me exists in your heart, or you would not have left me even the small cold remembrance you did. Louisa, has not some one misled you? Has not some one been talking to you who knows nothing of me or my affairs, putting into your head hard and calculating thoughts, unlike yourself?—you, who are the most generous and open-hearted of human beings? Write to me, and tell me all the truth, if it be but to relieve me from suspense. Tell me that you do not love me; that you left me because you are tired of me; that your note was written in pity to a cast-off lover! But I cannot believe it; *you* would not have acted thus. Then tell me, in Mercy's name, why you *did* go so singularly and so suddenly; and I will see if there be not a way and a means of seeing you again and banishing your doubts."

This letter, which was suitably closed and signed (and which I think should be inserted in "The Complete Letter-Writer," or otherwise it is not complete,) was a sore puzzle to her to whom it was addressed. How could she, how was she, to answer it? Her lover had not misjudged her in saying she was generous and candid; but what to do she knew not. How was she to tell the truth, or how forbear to tell it? Yet the letter made her very happy. Notwithstanding, she felt she must renounce all thought of marrying the author, and she wished to avoid a visit from him if possible. Not that she believed he would hesitate to marry her under any circumstances; how could she *now* think so? But with real love came all its accompaniments. She thought it would be a disadvantage to him; it might mortify his friends and family; lower him among his acquaintances, perhaps, or be a drag-weight to him in his career of ambition. Her resolution being taken, she willingly would have avoided his knowing how far beneath him she ranked in the scale of society; that artificial distinction, which is more binding on the conduct and feelings of mankind, from the prince to the peasant, than almost any passion or feeling of our nature; which will sometimes cause the miser to disregard his gold, the lover his heart, and even the Christian his conscience. That love is strong which can lose caste for the object of its love; that religion we acknowledge to be great and powerful which can make a man condescend to those of low degree. Why, this feeling will make a man, in certain circumstances, think he has done his neighbor a favor just by treating him politely!

Louisa wrote an answer, in which she exerted all her talents to console and please, and at the same time to forbid me hope. Vain task! Did she love me? I would compass sea and land to win her: difficulties only stimulated me. I little thought of the great gulf which separated us; the great gulf of very low station. Had I been a millionaire, I could indeed have built a golden bridge across it; but the peculiarity of differing grades is such, that, like similar electricities, the more nearly they approach the more certainly they repel each other. However, the time had not yet come to think of this. It is true I had learned that Louisa was poor; for, as may have been guessed, I had had a talk with Mrs. Moskey; but that lady had not chosen to be communicative beyond what suited her views, and the word "poor," connected with Louisa, to my mind ever represented genteel poverty—"fallen greatness."

Our correspondence continued for several weeks, until at last I with joy informed her that I had engaged in some business which would lead me to P——. How diligently I had sought it! What an interest I had taken in all matters likely to be transacted there!

Since the visit could not *now* be avoided, Louisa determined to do what was possible toward increasing the respectability of her family in those eyes which had become the world's to her. Her mother was astounded at the idea of a gentleman visitor. To work they went. Industry can do wonders, and art can do miracles. Some second-hand furniture was purchased at an auction, (Louisa preferred old and good to new and mean), more was solicited in payment of bad debts, and easily obtained. Soon there was a change. A carpet was spread over the floor, curtains were hung at the windows, sofas, chairs, tables, and all the etcetera of household furniture, were in due course provided; and among the items of a more genteel establishment they did not omit a servant. This latter was a negro girl, about fourteen years of age, whom they picked up in the neighborhood, and to drill whom, to the duties required of her, was both a task and an amusement. Tom was delighted by so many new things; and hope again, although with many misgiving checks, began to insinuate itself into the heart and cheek, the step and soul, of Louisa. Blithely again she sang at her work: again was her footstep light and her laugh merry.

Winter came on, bringing with it its extra expenses; and to unite economy with comfort, a fire was made in the parlor. Every evening a tow-cloth was spread before the improved Franklin-stove, the ironing-table set out, and there they cooked, and worked, and anticipated; always intending that when the company should come they would all be cleared away, and have the room comfortable to receive him. But, anxious to do as much as possible before that time, and the visitor delaying his coming, they daily continued, until fatigue obliged them to desist. The object being now to provide the utmost for the house in the shortest possible time, no outlays for other purposes were made. Cheerfully they denied themselves every luxury, and almost every comfort, beyond what was necessary to keep them in health. They looked not at butter, they dreamed not of meat; but they fatted on success in their main undertaking.

One evening it occurred to Louisa that her mother was an old woman, and ought not so to deny herself. It had been a cold, stormy day, such a one as it seemed most unlikely a stranger would arrive in, and she proposed to have a feast. Tom clapped his hands at the idea. They sent to the butcher's for some meat, and to the grocer's for eggs, tea and butter; and, the materials collected, the old woman set herself to her heart's delight, the cooking, while Louisa undertook to do up the ironing all by herself. They were all hard at work; the servant had gone to the pump for water; when lo! the long-expected knock at the door!

They regarded each other in ludicrous consternation. All thoughts were upon one object——to clear the room. The mother and daughter seized the ironing-table, and trotted it quickly into the back-room; ready-witted Tom threw the flat-irons, bread, meat, gridiron and kettle into the tow-cloth in one promiscuous huddle, and gathering up the four corners, dragged it after them. Louisa threw off her apron, and returned to the parlor as her mother just cleared the door with the remaining clutter, and the servant ushered in—myself.

I had arrived at the hotel about two hours before, and my first inquiry had been for the family; but the bar-keeper, not dreaming I could mean the washerwoman, knew of no such folks. I had wandered up one street and down another, in wet and wind, despairing in the fruitless endeavor to select from out the houses such as I imagined she must inhabit, the particular one which was her abode. From information previously obtained I knew I was in the right quarter of the town; yet to tell in which building a young lady lives, from the exterior of the same, is not a very promising undertaking, certainly; to question is better. But although I had tried both, I now determined to rely more especially upon the latter, and less upon my good judgment. Looking around for someone to interrogate, my attention was arrested by a negro girl who was paddling along through the wet with a bucket of water. It was the last glimmering of twilight, and she was the only person to be seen; so I accosted her: "My good girl, can you tell me where Mrs. Goldensoul lives?"

"Yes, Sir; I know where she lives. Is it Miss Louisa or the old woman you want to see? They axes fifty cents a dozen, I b'lieve, and do the mending too. It is very cheap!"

"What?" exclaimed I, no ray of the truth straying across my benighted intellect; "what do you say? I asked you if you could tell me where Mrs. Goldensoul lives. She has a daughter, Miss Louisa."

"Oh, may-be you're the gentleman! But they're uncommon busy to-night. Come along; I'll show you the way, Miss Lou. says the thermometer is below Jericho, and her mother shall eat one supper if there is not a clean shirt in martyrdom next Sunday morning! It'll do well enough for young folks that's smarty, but old women oughtn't to disembowel themselves, anyhow. Miss Lou. makes grammers, and her mother will call them crumpets; but she says she shall never be thrown up from the ways of ignorance. She don't want to wear the black silk and cap. She would rather go to bed. But them that's good enough for Miss Lou. is good enough for her mother."

By this time I had followed her up to the door of a dingy, most unprepossessing-looking house, which I inwardly hoped the increasing darkness mystified. I was out of patience, and quite sure there must be some mistake.

"You knock," said the girl, as she laid her hand upon the door, "while I go in and tell 'em he's come. She said I must not open the door until he knocks"; and setting her bucket down, she stepped inside, and holding the door by the merest crack ajar, stood peeping at me; waiting apparently to see if I would do as she had desired me. Accordingly, I knocked; whereupon she opened the door immediately, with a grin on her face that would have answered for a dozen welcomes. Her motions all indicated an inexplicable mixture of delight and embarrassment.

Hesitatingly she opened the parlor-door, and giving a peep in, said: "I think it's him. I couldn't keep him out any longer!" and vanished.

Within the house the scene was more in accordance with my preconceived ideas. Certain it was that Louisa was there, and my recent perplexities faded at once from my imagination. Never had the lady of my love seemed more beautiful or more charming; and I for a while forgot the world beside in the magic of her society. Presently she mentioned her mother; and although I earnestly wished that the old lady might be gone to lecture, I took the hint, and hoped I was to have the pleasure of seeing her. The laughing servant was instantly summoned with a small bell, and my message sent out. After a lapse of about a quarter of an hour, and when I had again forgotten there was such a being, she made her appearance—black silk and cap! and the negro girl's chat flashed through my mind, and gave me a spasmodic feeling similar to what the outside of the house had produced, only vastly more intense. Industry is a magician's wand, and had done a great deal; but it had not turned the hard-working old washer-woman into a fashionable lady.

Once in the street again, and out of Louisa's intoxicating presence, I began to reflect on what I had done, and what I was doing. Should I marry this girl? Pride answered "No!" And contemplating giving her up, I fancied I would never marry at all. Her brother, of whom she was so fond, should be a protegé of mine. I would do her all possible favors; and, in short, try very hard not to break her heart. And then my ideas became indistinct and confused, and wandered away into all sorts of impossibilities. I believed I would do anything, suffer anything, to alter the inexorable destiny which made me afraid and ashamed to make her my bride: which destiny was not so much a doubt of my ability to maintain her, as it was a belief that I could not do it in a certain style. I had thought also that my wife must be distinguished: I must be envied for her sake. Her family must be something to boast of. Mrs. Moskey was right: I had counted upon a market for my manly attractions, and Louisa could not pay the price. To be loved where I did love was not sufficient; it was not all I asked. Here was the difficulty which separated us.

But I did not reason thus at that time. No, I thought of what the world would say; of what my friends would say. "He has married the daughter of an old washer-woman!" The thought was intolerable. Whither would go my visions and hopes; my dreams of being distinguished and eminent? My vanity and self-conceit I should have looked after, but I did not. I thought (it is astonishing how like are all men to great characters!) of Bonaparte renouncing Josephine, and contrived to see an analogy between his greatness and mine. I thought of other great characters, who have cursed the world by their example. And then I thought of Adam, in the midst of Paradise, reaching out his hand to take the forbidden fruit. The analogy in this instance was not greater than in the other, save that I am sure he did not long for it more than I did for Louisa. At last I thought, and it was the most sensible thought which had occurred to me, that I was a rascal to think of abandoning her now. My whole course of conduct toward her passed in review before me, and forcibly enough returned to mind my first letter, and my assertion that Mrs. Moskey knew nothing of me or of my affairs. Did she not? Did I wish I had not said it? What had been my reply to her answer, telling me not to seek to see her again? Above all, what had been my conduct since? I had, as it were, forced her to confide in me: to desert her now would be base, mean, dastardly. Oddly enough, I was glad when I had come to this conclusion. If I had been guilty of consummate folly, I resolved at least that I would not add to it deliberate wickedness.

During this conflict of the passions of love and pride, I had arrived at my hotel. There lay, upon the mantle-piece of my room, a copy of the New Testament. Without reflection, I took it up, and opened accidentally to our SAVIOR's temptation, where Satan taketh him up into an exceeding high mountain, and showeth unto him all the kingdoms of this world, and the glory of them, and saith unto him: "All these things will I give thee, if thou wilt fall down and worship me." How forcible was the contrast to the thought recently in my mind! Adam, surrounded by every delight, fell for a single forbidden fruit; the SAVIOUR, hungry and solitary, was tempted with all this world can offer, and fell not. Yes, the kingdoms of this world, and the glory of them—these are our daily temptations; and for these we daily fall down and worship—ay, the Devil. And was I not in the very act of doing him homage when I would so ill-treat that lovely and unprotected, girl? Yes, and tear out my own heart also, to lay it a sacrifice upon his worldly altar! I felt disgusted with myself. I resolved again to do, otherwise—to do better.

The next day I saw Louisa again, and as I had had some work to do to bring myself to a right conclusion, so had I still more to make her consent to our immediate union; for with the usual consistency of a human being, I, who the day before did not believe I would marry her at all, now declared that my prosperity depended on this last proposition. My determination being taken, I had resolved at once that they could not too soon, for my pride, quit their present mode of life, and I well knew it could not be done in any other way.

All my plans of life were now changed; or rather it became necessary for me to have a plan, and not to dream any more. And first I wrote to my mother a full account of what I had done, and received for reply: "My son, be always honorable, just and generous, and you will be always right." Also came a letter from my brother, saying: "Dear Fred., I understand you are about to be married to a very worthy girl, a bricklayer's daughter. (I had, in my account to the family, substituted the father's occupation for the mother's.) I hope you will prove yourself worthy of her. Moreover, I intend that this, my reply to your letter, shall gain me a considerable number of votes, and beg you will speak of it accordingly; it will not interfere with your own capital. I believe you are a cunning fellow, and I have a great mind to envy you your luck. Had my father been a wood sawyer, or my mother a washer-woman, or myself a blacksmith, I believe I could have won my last election. Yours, Frank." Thus was the first great bug-bear of my imagination, what would my family say, answered. As for the world in general, they did not send in their opinions in writing.

My next business was to hire an office in P——, and look me out a respectable house, both of which I furnished as well as the means at my disposal would permit, feeling all the while as if I had renounced the world, which means that I believed the world would certainly renounce me.

And Louisa and I were married. After which I had insisted that my mother-in-law should no longer work for the public. "No, Lou.," said I, "if I cannot make out to maintain you all, you must be content to starve with me." "Nobody will know it," urged the old woman. But I insisted strenuously that no such idea should be for an instant entertained; and making it a matter of personal favor to myself; my wishes were acceded to. I hired a carriage to take us all, after the wedding, to our new home; whereupon Mrs. G. and Tom were of opinion that Louisa's castle of fancy had come down to her, so great was their sense of elevation. It was now their turn to talk, while Louisa and I were silent. For us, although no pomp of circumstance attended our simple wedding, there was deep and heartfelt happiness. I had acted rightly and honorably, in my own estimation, (oh, the blessing of a clear conscience!) and I was married to a woman whom I felt that I loved as I never could have loved again any other upon earth. No, not although I had found another as beautiful and as talented, which was scarcely to be looked for, with wealth and friends, and all to boast, another would not have been the same; another would not have been my first love. And with these reflections there came a sense of manliness and independence, which actually seemed to expand my frame, and made me feel more like a man than ever I had felt before in my life. If there rested a shadow of anxiety upon my feelings, it was a fear that I might not have success in my business, and that what I had said in my haste would even prove a prophecy, and they would have to starve with me. How little I knew the world indeed!

I was earnestly attentive to my business. I associated with men of business, and to business alone I applied myself. My home was the abode of neatness and cheerfulness. What bright smiles ever greeted me there!

What devoted hearts sought my comfort! I was a happy man. My business increased; and when at the end of a year I settled up my accounts, I found that so far from being in debt my income had exceeded my expenses. As for my clothes, one of the blessings of the Israelites seemed suddenly to befall some of them; my shirts did not wax old, nor my stockings wear out, for the garments, which were always mended, seemed never to wear out. How white was the linen washed by such careful hands! How sweet, how healthful the viands, where affection plead for economy, and economy was influenced by affection! In every part of my domestic establishment did devoted love show its superiority to careless wealth. How could I do otherwise than grow rich, with my interests so carefully attended to? My acquaintances thought it worth their while to notice my wife. My constituents boasted of my independence; and not without reason, for my eyes were opened to the real independence of an American citizen; to the nobility of birth, indeed the born of noble hearts; not of wealthy manors, not of lordly titles! My mother-in-law has become reconciled to her black silk and cap; and the kind-hearted, clever old soul, has nursed me through so many bad colds, and helped me through so many trifling dilemmas, that I have come to think her cheerful face and sound sense quite as valuable as a fashionable air. Tom has gone to college, and Louisa rides in her carriage, holding as distinguished a position as wealth and real merit can bestow. As adversity did not sour their tempers, so neither has prosperity hardened their hearts. That religion which was the support of the former caused the latter to overflow with good deeds, which are all the more judiciously planned and executed from the experience of privation and the practical knowledge of the ways and means of the poor. They have not thought it necessary to forget the friends and acquaintances of their obscurity; and their universal affability, and particular good opinion of myself, has added its quantum to my present popularity, so that, for my especial benefit, I do not know where I could have found a more influential family. And I myself have the comfortable reflection, that I neither courted the rich nor ill-treated the poor to win my present prosperity.

APPENDIX B

Other Unpublished Manuscripts of Ellen Brown Anderson and Corinna Brown Aldrich

Many of the letters that Ellen and Corinna wrote to their brother Mannevillette discuss their writing projects and attempts at publication. The sisters left behind a number of manuscripts, including several stories and fragments, which have been passed down through their descendants and remain in the possession of living family members. The family generously made these manuscripts available to me. Corinna apparently refers to one of these stories in an August 1836 letter to Mannevillette revealing that the sisters had begun working on a new novel. Unfortunately, they were forced to abandon the project to take care of sick relatives, but a partial draft that might be the first chapter of this story remains. This seventeen-page manuscript, titled *Sketches of Life During the Second Seminole War*, consists of a single chapter subtitled "The Elopement."[1] Also among these manuscripts is a forty-five-page story fragment by E.M.A. (Ellen Maria Anderson), "A Panic in the Hotel Disclosing the Shocking State of Capt. Fitz Ogle's Affections." Set primarily in the Devilmacare Hotel in New York City, this story includes plot and character elements resembling those of *Sketches of Life During the Second Seminole War*, notably a scandalous elopement and a dissipated captain, but it too is incomplete.

Among these manuscripts, the only complete story is "Aspirations After Gentility," set in the village of Stone Mountain, Georgia. This 114-page story, written by Corinna, Ellen, or both sisters, features Mrs. Muttermuch, a pompous social climber from an Atlantic state, and her daughters, who vacation at a log cabin resort. It includes detailed descriptions of Stone Mountain, the surrounding countryside, and the resort, and it provides local color in the dialogue of the simple rural folk who live around the village and operate the resort. This story is a social satire focused on pretentious city-dwellers, but it mostly bypasses the opportunity to engage its southern regional setting imaginatively.

These stories criticize the world of mannered society and its pretensions but present this criticism in a lighthearted satiric tone. *The Storm* also displays elements of gentle satire, as in Jenny's description of the island's social elite, who had moved there from all over the country to get rich. For example, Jenny remarks that "there were fashionable ladies from New York and other cities, and very flashy ones from everywhere. These all met and danced in common, and abused each other with charming cordiality" (45). Overall, however, compared to the sisters' other writings, the criticism of personal vices in *The Storm* is heavier, as in the depiction of Peter Greenough's immoral behavior and severe punishment, and the tone of *The Storm* is more serious, the social criticism focusing directly on the restricted position of women in American society.

The following is a description of Brown family manuscripts currently in possession of the editor; the essays probably were all written by Ellen when she was attempting to establish a writing career in New York in the 1850s:

I. Fiction

A. ~~A Panic in the Hotel Disclosing the~~ Shocking ~~State of Capt. Fitz Ogle's Affections~~

By E.M.A. [Ellen Maria Anderson]

[45 pages, sewn together neatly, on 12" × 3¾" lined paper; all pages intact with few blemishes except for page 4, torn in half; writing only on front of paper; neatly penned]

B. Aspirations after Gentility [Ellen Anderson]

By O. N. E.

[9½ × 7½ lined paper; 114 pages front and back of 57 sheets, sewn together; opening setting is a locomotive coming to a stop at Stone Mountain resort in Georgia]

C. Sketches of Life in Florida During The Seminole War [Ellen Anderson?]

Chap. 1

The Elopement

[17 pages, front and back, 9½ × 7½ sheets; watermark C BUNCE MANCHESTER CT]

II. Essays

A. Chat with Fame

E.M.A.

[31 pages, front and back of 9½ × 7½ lined paper; many corrections & additions]

B. Translation of a Pamphlet titled
"New Route for an inter Oceanic Communication
Documents relative to a reconnaissance
Of the River A[?] or P[?]
Which empties into the Great Ocean
Puebla
1851"
[on page 29, signed] Ivan B Ardit[?]
Felicite Ardit
[31 pages, front and back of blueish 9½ × 7¼ lined paper, bound with shoestring-sized cord]

C. Imitations of Spooner
[unsigned, but clearly Ellen; 3 pages front only, 8 × 4¼ unlined, gilt-edged paper with Windsor Hills watermark or stamped emblem; political argument against the inclusion of slaves under the Declaration of Independence or the Constitution.]

D. The New Method of Reform [Ellen Anderson]
[5 pages of same paper as I. C. above; essay criticizing would-be reformers of prostitutes.]

E. Thoughts on the Influence of Novels
By the Condensationalist [Ellen Anderson]
[12 × 7¾ paper, 6 sheets; 1st sheet watermark: O.W.F. & HURLEUI SO. Lee MASS; 12 pages front and back with one rough sheet sewn on; the last 1 & ½ page is in pencil; essay on the appeal of novels to love and vanity; basically argues that novel reading is harmful.]

F. England and her Volunteers [Ellen Anderson?] [penciled date: Feb. '60; 12 × 7½ front only of four sheets; watermark EAGLE MILLS SUFFIELD; essay against England's raising an army to attack the U.S.]

Note

1 See the introduction to this book, 21–23, for more about this story fragment.

APPENDIX C

The Storm, True Womanhood, Feminism, and Companionate Marriage in Key West

The Storm explores issues related to education, marriage, and the position of women in mid-nineteenth-century America.[1] This novella's opening quotation, which comes from William Cowper's "Pairing-Time Anticipated" (1795), announces the story's focus: "Choose not alone a proper mate / But proper time to marry" (*The Storm* 1). Its female narrator, Jenny Mansfield, tells the story of her first marriage as Jenny Greenough, *The Storm*'s protagonist, and examines ideas and attitudes concerning marriage along with the closely related subject of education for women. *The Storm* challenges accepted gender practices prevalent in antebellum America, particularly roles shaped by the concept of the "separate spheres" and the ideal of the "True Woman" and "True Womanhood." In a 1966 article, Barbara Welter explains that "in the cult of True Womanhood presented by the women's magazines, gift annuals and religious literature of the nineteenth century" (151), the ideal of the True Woman consisted of four primary attributes "by which a woman judged herself and was judged by her husband, her neighbors, and society: 'piety, purity, submissiveness, and domesticity'" (151–52). As Mary Louise Roberts confirms in 2002, "Historians continue to agree that 'true womanhood' was the centerpiece of nineteenth-century female identity" (150).

As the reality of her marriage becomes clear, Jenny increasingly resists the constraints of her role in the separate spheres and by a twist of fortune is freed from the cage of True Womanhood. Although the reader gets only a glimpse of her second marriage, it clearly embodies most aspects of a different ideal, the companionate marriage. Anya Jabour explains the concepts of the Companionate Marriage: "By the early nineteenth century, many women and men had placed a new value on affectionate ties between family members, particularly within the immediate family, whose nucleus was a married couple joined by romantic love" (2). This newer notion challenged "the ideology of 'separate spheres'" in which "men devoted their lives to self-advancement; [and] women looked for fulfillment in self-sacrifice" (Jabour 2–3). The inner struggle of Jenny Greenough reflects the tension among all of these conflicting beliefs as women considered their own place, or places, in American society. The mid-century island of Key West, with a diverse community of residents and visitors from assorted classes, regions, and nations, provides a perfect setting for this confluence of ideas: as Jenny Mansfield comments, "We were people met accidentally in a strange place. We were on business—to make fortunes. We would amuse ourselves a little, finish our business, and return to society and civilization" (*The Storm* 37).

This mixture of beliefs and attitudes about marriage and women's place in nineteenth-century American society plays out in the narrative as Jenny Mansfield revisits her past, when at age sixteen, she married Peter Greenough, a twenty-nine-year-old physician who takes his young bride from New York to Key West to accompany him as he seeks his fortune. As was the case for most girls in the United States during the mid-nineteenth century, Jenny's limited education prepared her for only one thing: marriage. The narrator explains that her parents, "in conjunction with the rest of the world, believed that a young woman was born, destined, fore-ordained and commissioned to get married" (*The Storm* 4). Jenny reveals that "no objection was made to the gentleman who stood to me in the position of husband and protector" (*The Storm* 3). As Barbara Welter remarks, the True Woman "feels herself weak and timid. She needs a protector" (159). Peter eagerly grasps the man's role in the public sphere as provider, "intend[ing] to be rich in an incredibly short space of time" (5). As Jenny recognizes, her appointed role within the woman's domestic sphere is to support his pursuits: "Did I not determine to be a help meet for him! With what zeal I looked forward to my new duties of housekeeper and wife!" (*The Storm* 6).

Peter Greenough fully embraces his unrestricted role in the man's sphere, as was his privilege in the strict antebellum patriarchy. Key West naturally attracted Peter, a man chasing "speedy wealth and daring adventure," with its atmosphere of "freedom from restraint" (*The Storm* 10). Welter shows that nineteenth-century men were thought to be constantly "exposed to conflict and evil" (172), and indeed, even while on the ship to Key West, Peter begins to succumb to the temptations that allegedly beset men: "He would get cross, and swear out of those fine mustaches of his, and would go down in the cabin, and play cards by the hour, and drink" rum and then lie about it to Jenny (*The Storm* 17–18).

Once Jenny and Peter settle into their Key West home, Jenny attempts to fulfill the role she has been trained for, that of the True Woman to her husband. Unfortunately, she soon begins to have concerns about the condition of their marriage when she discovers Peter in suspicious circumstances at the house of their neighbor, Mrs. Cantwell, and overhears Peter demean Jenny as "a mere doll" (*The Storm* 40). When Jenny unexpectedly confronts them as they engage in this conversation about her, he takes her home and actually chastises her, declaring openly to Jenny that she is a child compared to Mrs. Cantwell, who is a woman, and demands that Jenny keep herself at home, the proper place for a woman according to the separate spheres doctrine. As strange as this scene may appear to a modern reader, from a typical nineteenth-century American's perspective, Peter's remarks are appropriate; he was simply reminding Jenny of her designated subordinate place in their marriage and of her assigned space in the home. Defending the submissive, childlike role for married women, Sarah Jane Clarke—speaking through the persona of Grace Greenwood—remarked in her 1850 *Greenwood Leaves*, "True feminine genius is ever timid, doubtful, clingingly dependent; a perpetual childhood" (310). Barbara Welter asserts, "Submission was perhaps the most feminine virtue expected of woman" (158). Jenny therefore abides by Peter's wishes, accusing herself of "folly and unkindness" (*The Storm* 41); here also, Jenny adheres to the True Womanhood ideal. According to Welter, women who failed to live up to the standards of True Womanhood often blamed themselves (174). After this confrontation, Jenny spends several weeks completely confined and isolated within her home, pining away for company in the evenings while Peter supposedly engages in business. Once again, Jenny's situation fits the pattern for true married women within the social world of the two spheres. Welter explains that "woman, in the cult of True Womanhood . . . was the hostage in the home" (151). Peter neglects Jenny while he enjoys the company of others, including Mrs. Cantwell, and he dismisses Jenny's needs and concerns. When she decides one evening to accept a social invitation, Peter jealously persuades her instead to stay home with him but thereafter continues to abandon her in the evenings, leaving her imprisoned in her solitary reveries. Often, Jenny retreats to her mosquito tent, a sanctuary that represents her restricted place in the marriage.

Although Jenny strives to fulfill the duties of a True Woman, she begins to want her marriage to be more of a companionate marriage, such as was becoming widespread in northern states, including her native New York. She recalls her early preparations for marriage: "I had been taught to think that romance ended when one settled down into married life" (*The Storm* 1). Jenny attempts to overcome these low expectations: "All in my nature which could be called affection was concentrated and bestowed upon him" (*The Storm* 19–20). Jenny wants to be "a companion to my husband, [but] I was simply a pet" (*The Storm* 49). Jenny guiltily finds herself daydreaming about the kind of man who could truly love her, but she admits to herself that "when this became my state of feeling, I seemed to lose my value" (20).

After an argument with Peter during the journey to Key West, Jenny is comforted by looking over the vessel's side and enjoying "how beautifully and wonderfully this world was constructed, light and beauty breaking through everywhere, and [I] wondered why young women could not be allowed to go about and admire it, without a protector, as our husbands call themselves" (16–17). Jenny's realization comes at a moment of confluence of several intellectual streams of Romanticism: reverence for external nature, assertion of individual independence, and rejection of social restrictions. Jenny now begins to question the patriarchal society that restricts her personal freedom of movement and has bound her into an early, unsatisfying marriage without preparing her for any other role. As a result, Jenny feels discontent with the limitations of her own education, and of the education of women in general, a feeling that intensifies throughout the story. After moving into her new home, Jenny painfully recognizes the failure of her education: "That a young woman should be properly qualified to superintend a kitchen, and keep a house, was in the estimation of my mother, the only preparation necessary to fit her to be married. In that respect I was thought to be well educated. The text-book principally used in my instruction had been *The American Housewife*" (*The Storm* 27).[2]

Elsewhere, Jenny complains openly about the education offered to girls; she remarks in a conversation with the lighthouse keeper, "It seems to me, we women never have a chance to mature. . . . It is the fashion to take us from school at sixteen and seventeen, and set us about getting married, whereas boys of the same age are put at school, trade, or business, and the hardest kind of study." She adds, "I wish I had been a different person" (53). When Philip Mansfield, the lighthouse keeper's twenty-two-year-old son and her future husband, asks her, "Why don't you read?" She remains silent, but the narrator, Jenny Mansfield looking back on this scene, responds, "I did read. It seemed to me that reading did not answer the purpose" (53). Jenny clearly is formulating feminist ideas, though she does not use the term "feminist."[3] Jenny Greenough's newly developed, unconventional opinions about her constrained role as a woman closely resemble those expressed by *The Storm*'s likely author, Ellen Brown Anderson, whose letters voice frustration over poor education, training, and opportunities for women.

A chance opportunity arises that changes Jenny's life: she accepts a last-minute offer from her brother-in-law to travel with him via steamship from Key West to New York to visit her parents. A startling series of dramatic events occurs on this journey: the ship explodes, a stranger rescues Jenny in the dark, her brother-in-law dies, she luckily catches a ride on another ship to New York, and she learns Christian gratitude for being spared (63–64). Armed with this new religious faith—a necessary tool for a True Woman—she arrives safely in New York and listens to her mother's admonition that "a wife should never quit her husband" (64). She begins to believe her mother and therefore heads back home to Peter.

She arrives in Key West as the storm approaches the island and soon discovers that her house is abandoned and closed up, and the net—the symbol of her entrapment in an oppressive, unsatisfying marriage—is gone. The hurricane spectacularly lashes the island, but Philip Mansfield, who had by happy coincidence been a passenger on the very ship that returned her to Key West, rescues her heroically with his "two strong arms." When the storm subsides, she discovers that her faithless husband and her faithless sister, Melinda, had left the island together that morning—on a ship bound not for New York but for England.

As the tale reaches its conclusion, the feminist strains mostly disappear as the gothic romance mode and a conventional marriage plot take over. Jenny faces the sublime forces of nature at their mightiest when the storm floods the island, destroys her house along with most of the island's other structures, rips coffins from their graves, and flings corpses in terrifying poses across the landscape. After she discovers the bodies of Melinda and Peter on the shore, she falls into a several-weeks-long feverish swoon worthy of an Ann Radcliffe heroine. Freed from her marriage by fate and the forces of nature, Jenny can live on her own terms, and she chooses a largely conventional path. When she recovers from her lengthy faint and illness and Philip recovers from the loss of his family in the storm, Jenny thanks him for saving her—twice: "for the same arms which saved me in the storm, were those which rescued me from the cabin of the steam boat. . . . I knew it when you bore me through the storm" (88).

They leave Key West forever and move to New York; Philip goes into business and becomes successful, and they marry, giving this story a predictable and perhaps unsatisfying ending. Still, Jenny has learned from the experience of her premature and unfulfilling first marriage and from her musings over her own limited status as a woman; plus, Philip is undoubtedly a better man than was Peter. Jenny will have a happier life in her second marriage, which does have some distinctly progressive elements. After she marries Philip, Jenny pursues her quest for more education, plunging into a regimen of "reading and study" (89). Moreover, Philip and Jenny do not settle for the conventional, restrictive pattern of separate spheres but instead work together to achieve a companionate marriage: rather than staying at home to supervise the household while her husband makes his way in the world, Jenny travels to foreign lands with him, and she comes to believe that no "other charm was greater to him than my own influence" (89). Jenny's stormy first marriage and her more companionate second marriage have taught her "that deep and strong affection is found only in sensible and stable persons" (90)—and that wise observation concludes *The Storm*.

Notes

1 Copyright © 2017 College English Association. This article first appeared in *CEA Critic* 79, no. 3 (November 2017). Published with permission by Johns Hopkins University Press.
2 See note 10, page 82.
3 Interestingly, the term "feminist," meaning "of, relating to, or advocating the rights and equality of women," first appeared in a publication in 1852, about the time when *The Storm* was written (*OED*).

WORKS CITED AND CONSULTED

I. Unpublished manuscripts, letters, emails

Alexander, Elizabeth. Letter to John J. Traynor Jr. May 8, 1972. Photocopy in the editor's possession.

[Aldrich, Corinna Brown, and Ellen Brown Anderson?] "Aspirations After Gentility." Unpublished manuscript in the editor's possession.

[Aldrich, Corinna Brown, and Ellen Brown Anderson?] *Sketches of Life During the Second Seminole War*. Unpublished manuscript in the editor's possession.

Anderson, Ellen Maria. "A Panic in the Hotel Disclosing the Shocking State of Capt. Fitz Ogle's Affections." Unpublished manuscript in the editor's possession.

Anderson-Brown Papers. United States Military Academy, West Point, New York. Microfilm copy of the collection in the editor's possession.

Gill, Raymond. Email to Keith Huneycutt. May 6, 2018.

Goolsby, Louis. Letter to John J. Traynor Jr. February 25, 1973. Photocopy in the editor's possession.

La Coe, Norman. "Introduction to *The Storm*." Unpublished typescript. May 14, 1991. P. K. Yonge Library of Florida History, Special Collections, Gainesville, Florida. Photocopy in the editor's possession.

La Coe, Norman. Letter to Keith L. Huneycutt. September 6, 2016. In the editor's possession.

La Coe, Norman. Letter to John J. Traynor Jr. May 1, 1972. Photocopy in the editor's possession.

La Coe, Norman. Letter to John J. Traynor Jr. October 12, 1972. Photocopy in the editor's possession.

The Storm. N.d. MS. Special and Area Collections of the P. K. Yonge Library of Florida History, George A. Smathers Libraries. University of Florida, Gainesville.

Traynor, Elizabeth. Email to Keith Huneycutt. February 27, 2021.

Traynor, John L. Letter to Norman La Coe. May 6, 1972. Photocopy in the editor's possession.

II. Books, Stories, and Articles

Abel, Elizabeth, Marianne Hirsch, and Elizabeth Langland, eds. *The Voyage In: Fictions of Female Development*. Hanover, N.H.: University Press of New England, 1983.

The American Housewife: Containing the Most Valuable and Original Receipts in all the Various Branches of Cookery, and Written in a Minute and Methodical Manner: Together with a Collection of Miscellaneous Receipts and Directions Relative to Housewifery: Also The Whole Art of Carving. New York: Collins, Keese. 6th ed. 1841. Google Books: https://www.google.com/books/edition/The_American_Housewife/o3MEAAAAYAAJ?kptab=editions&gbpv=1.

Aldrich, Corinna Brown. "The Grumble Family." *The Philadelphia Saturday Chronicle*, June 3, 1837. Microfilm. American Jewish Historical Society. Accessed via scanned image September 6, 2023.

Anderson, Ellen Brown. "A Novel in a Nut-Shell." *The Knickerbocker*, September, 1850. 215–231. Google Books: https://www.google.com/books/edition/The_Knickerbocker/5sFOAQAAMAAJ?hl=en&gbpv=1&dq=Knickerbocker,+September,+1850&pg=PA205&printsec=frontcover.

Audubon, John James, and William MacGillivray. *Ornithological Biography, or, An account of the Habits of the Birds of the United States of America: Accompanied by Descriptions of the Objects Represented in the Work Entitled The Birds of America and Interspersed with Delineations of American Scenery and Manners*. Vol. 3, E. L. Carey & and A. Hart, 1832–1839. *Sabin Americana: History of the Americas, 1500–1926.* Accessed June 27, 2022: link.gale.com/apps/doc/CY0108480464/SABN?u=lake33936&sid=bookmark-SABN&xid=db7eab84&pg=173.

Barnes, Jay. *Florida's Hurricane History*. Chapel Hill: University of North Carolina Press, 1998. Print.

Baruch, E. H. "The Feminine Bildungsroman: Education Through Marriage." *Massachusetts Review* 22: 335–57.

Beecher, Catherine Esther. *An Essay on Slavery and Abolitionism, with Reference to the Duty of American Females*. Philadelphia, 1837. *Sabin Americana*. Gale, Cengage Learning. Florida Southern College. Accessed January 6, 2017: http://galenet.galegroup.com/servlet/Sabin?af=RN&ae=CY105406568&srchtp=a&ste=14.

Bennett, Kelsey L. *Principle and Propensity: Experience and Religion in the Nineteenth-Century British and American Bildungsroman*. Columbia: University of South Carolina Press, 2014.

Benstock, Shari, et al. *A Handbook of Literary Feminisms*. New York: Oxford University Press, 2002. Print.

Bird, Robert Montgomery. *The Adventures of Robin Day*. Philadelphia: Lee & Blanchard, 1839. Print.

Brown, Canter. *Ossian Bingley Hart: Florida's Loyalist Reconstruction Governor*. Baton Rouge: Louisiana State University Press, 1997. Print.

Browne, Jefferson B. *Key West: The Old and The New*. St. Augustine: The Record Company; Printers and Publishers. 1912; reprint, Gainesville: University of Florida Press, 1973. Print.

Buckley, Jerome Hamilton. *Season of Youth: The Bildungsroman from Dickens to Golding*. Cambridge, Mass.: Harvard University Press, 1974. Print.

Condit, Cyrus Parkhurst. *A Trip to Florida for Health and Sport: The Lost 1855 novel of Cyrus Parkhurst Conduit*. Edited and with an introduction by Maurice O'Sullivan and Wenxian Zhang. The Florida Historical Society Press, 2009. Print.

Cooper, James Fenimore. *Jack Tier: Or the Florida Reef*. 2 vols. New York: Burgess, Stringer & Co., 1848. Print.

Corey, Michael. "Understanding the Key West Hurricane of 1846." *Florida Keys Seritage Journal* 20, no. 4 (Summer 2010): 1–16. Print.

Courtney, Rosemary. "M.E.D. Brown, (1810–1896): American Lithographer and Painter." *American Art Journal* 12, no. 4 (Autumn 1980): 66–77. Print.

Cowper, William. "Pairing Time Anticipated, Moral" (lines 64–65). In *The Poems of William Cowper.* Vol. 2. Chiswick: Press of C. Whittinham, College House, 1822. Accessed May 27, 2023: https://www.google.com/books/edition/The_poems_of_William_Cowper_The_life_of/soE4_kKIoWwC?hl=en&gbpv=1&dq=Cowper,+William.+%E2%80%9CPairing+Time+Anticipated%22&pg=PA213&printsec=frontcover.

Curtis, George William, and Augustus Hoppin. *The Potiphar Papers.* G. P. Putnam, 1853. *Sabin Americana: History of the Americas, 1500–1926.* Accessed June 10, 2022: link.gale.com/apps/doc/CY0102963173/SABN?u=lake33936&sid=bookmark-SABN&xid=2f395b9c&pg=1.

Cusick, James. Blog post: https://ufspecialcollections.wordpress.com/2017/01/23/blog-post-title-3/.

Davis, Thadious M. "Women's Art and Authorship in the Southern Region: Connections." In *The Female Tradition in Southern Literature* ed. Carol S. Manning, 15–36. Champaign: University of Illinois Press, 1993. Print.

Denham, James M. *A Rogue's Paradise: Crime and Punishment in Antebellum Florida, 1821–1861.* Tuscaloosa: University of Alabama Press, 1997. Print.

Denham, James M., and Keith L. Huneycutt, eds. *Echoes from a Distant Frontier: The Brown Sisters' Correspondence from Antebellum Florida, 1835–1850.* Columbia: University of South Carolina Press, 2004. Print.

———. "'Everything Is Hubbub Here': Lt. James Willoughby Anderson's Seminole War, 1837–1842." *Florida Historical Quarterly* 82, no. 3 (Winter 2004): 313–59. Print.

———. *The Letters of George Long Brown: A Yankee Merchant on Florida's Antebellum Frontier.* Gainesville: University Press of Florida, 2019. Print.

———. "Our Desired Haven: The Letters of Corinna Brown Aldrich from Antebellum Key West, 1849–1850." *Florida Historical Quarterly* (Spring 2001): 517–45. Print.

———. "With Scott in Mexico: Letters of Captain James W. Anderson in the Mexican War, 1846–1847." *Journal of the Military History of the West* (Spring 1998): 19–48. Print.

Dobson, Joanne. "The American Renaissance Reenvisioned." In *The (Other) American Traditions: Nineteenth-century Women Writers,* ed. Warren. New Brunswick, N.J.: Rutgers University Press, 1993. Online.

Dodd, Dorothy. "The Wrecking Business on the Florida Reef." *Florida Historical Quarterly* 22 (April 1944): 171–99. Print.

Dodd, William G. "Early Education in Tallahassee and the West Florida Seminary, Now Florida State University." *Florida Historical Quarterly* 27, no. 2 (1948): 157–80. JSTOR, Accessed June 28, 2022: http://www.jstor.org/stable/30138720. Online.

Dolin, Eric Jay. *A Furious Sky: The Five-Hundred-Year History of America's Hurricanes.* New York: Liveright, 2020. Print.

Donaldson, Madelaine H. (Everett). *The Thrilling Narrative and Extraordinary Adventures of Miss Madelaine H. Everett who Was Abducted from the Bloomington Ladies' Seminary in Florida; and After Passing Through the Most Wonderful and Painful Scenes, Was Finally Rescued by Her Friends at an Auction Mart in Havana Where She Was About to Be Sold as a Slave*. Philadelphia: Barclay & Co., 1859. Google Books. https://play.google.com/books/reader?id=yAQnAAAAMAAJ&pg=GBS.PA3&hl=en.

"Dreadful Calamity of the Hudson River." *New York Times*, July 29, 1852. https://timesmachine.nytimes.com/timesmachine/1852/07/30/87838967.html?pageNumber=1.

Evans, Augusta Jane. *Beulah*. Edited with an introduction by Elizabeth Fox-Genovese. Baton Rouge: Louisiana State University Press, 1992. Print.

Franklin, Wayne. *James Fenimore Cooper: The Later Years*. New Haven, Conn.: Yale University Press, 2017. EBSCOhost, https://search.ebscohost.com/login.aspx?direct=true&AuthType=shib&db=nlebk&AN=1494444&site=eds-live&scope=site.

Gallagher, Catherine. *Nobody's Story: The Vanishing Acts of Women Writers in the Marketplace, 1670–1920*. Berkeley: University of California Press, 1995. EBSCOhost, search.ebscohost.com/login.aspx?direct=true&AuthType=shib&db=nlebk&AN=19219&site=eds-live&scope=site.

Gannon, Michael, ed. *The New History of Florida*. Gainesville: University Press of Florida, 1996. Print.

Gardner, Janette C. *An Annotated Bibliography of Florida Fiction, 1801–1980*. Preface by James A. Servies. St. Petersburg, Fla.: Little Bayou Press, 1983. Print.

Gould, Hannah Flagg. "The Pirate of Key West." In *The New Monthly Belle Assemblée: A Magazine of Literature and Fiction* 25 (August 1846): 224–34. Google Books. https://books.google.com/books?id=Z0UFAAAAQAAJ&pg=PA224&dq=%22The+Pirate+of+Key+West%22&hl=en&newbks=1&newbks_redir=0&sa=X&ved=2ahUKEwjU9MuhvP74AhULF1kFHVWFBzYQ6AF6BAgGEAI#v=onepage&q=%22The%20Pirate%20of%20Key%20West%22&f=false.

Greenwood, Grace. *Greenwood Leaves: A Collection of Sketches and Letters*. Boston: Tickner, Reed, and Fields, 1850. *Sabin Americana*. Gale, Cengage Learning. Florida Southern College. Accessed June 21, 2017: http://galenet.galegroup.com/servlet/Sabin?af=RN&ae=CY102926839&srchtp=a&ste=14.

Hardin, James N. *Reflection and Action: Essays on the Bildungsroman*. Columbia: University of South Carolina Press, 1991. Print.

Harris, Susan K. "'But Is It any Good?': Evaluating Nineteenth-Century American Women's Fiction." In *The (Other) American Traditions: Nineteenth-century Women Writers*, ed. Warren. New Brunswick, N.J.: Rutgers University Press, 1993. Online.

Hentz, Caroline Lee. *The Banished Son and Other Stories of the Heart*. Philadelphia: T. B. Peterson, 1852. Google Books. https://play.google.com/books/reader?id=NKQcAAAAMAAJ&pg=GBS.PA6&hl=en.

———. *Marcus Warland: Or, The Long Moss Spring; A Tale of the South*. Philadelphia: A. Hart, 1852. Google Books: https://play.google.com/books/reader?id=xqEuAAAAYAAJ&pg=GBS.PP1&hl=en.

Herbert, Henry William. *Ringwood the Rover: A Tale of Florida*. Philadelphia: W. H. Graham, 1843. *Sabin Americana: History of the Americas, 1500–1926*. Accessed July 16, 2022: link.gale.com/apps/doc/CY0102014076/SABN?u=lake33936&sid=bookmark-SABN&xid=e127ef5f&pg=1.

Huneycutt, Keith L. "The Brown Sisters in Antebellum Florida: Florida Writers?" *Florida Studies: Proceedings of the 2005 Annual Meeting of the Florida College English Association* 1 (2006): 75–80. Print.

———. "*The Storm*: The Case for Ellen Brown Anderson's Authorship." In *Florida Studies Review*, ed. Allyson D. Marino, and Marcy L. Galbreath, 20–32. Cambridge: Cambridge Scholars Publishing, 2018. Print.

———. "*The Storm*: True Womanhood, Feminism, and Companionate Marriage in Antebellum Key West." *College English Association Critic* 79, no. 3 (November 2017): 291–98. Copyright © 2017. The College English Association. This article first appeared in *The CEA Critic* 79, no. 3 (November 2017): 291–98. Print.

Ide, Laura E. "Bookseller O. J. Briskey Still Missed in Micanopy." *Ocala Star-Banner*. December 14, 2014. https://www.ocala.com/article/LK/20141231/News/604149989/OS.

Jabour, Anya. *Marriage in the Early Republic: Elizabeth and William Wirt and the Companionate Ideal*. Baltimore, Md.: Johns Hopkins University Press, 1998. Print.

Judson, Edward Zane Carroll. *The Red Revenger: or, The Pirate King of the Floridas; A Romance of the Gulf and Its Islands*. By Ned Buntline (pseud.). New York: Samuel French, 1847. Google Books. https://play.google.com/books/reader?id=ePRLAQAAMAAJ&pg=GBS.PA10&hl=en

———. *Matanzas: or, A Brother's Revenge; A Tale of Florida*. By Ned Buntline (pseud.). Boston: G. H. Williams, 1848. Google Books. https://play.google.com/books/reader?id=7D0gAQAAMAAJ&pg=GBS.PA2&hl=en

Kearney, Kevin E., and William Marvin. "Autobiography of William Marvin." *Florida Historical Quarterly* 36, no. 3 (1958): 179–222. JSTOR. Accessed July 17, 2022: http://www.jstor.org/stable/30139043.

Kemp, Bill. "Major's Female College Was an Early Bloomington School for Young Women." *Pantagraph*. March 25, 2012, updated June 25, 2013. https://pantagraph.com/news/local/major-s-female-college-was-an-early-bloomington-school-for-young-women/article_350e8866-75fc-11e1-93d0-0019bb2963f4.html.

Love, Harold. *Attributing Authorship: An Introduction*. Cambridge: Cambridge University Press, 2002. Print.

Makala, Jeffrey. "The Spencerian and Palmer Methods." In *Born to Please: The Art of Handwriting Instruction*. University of South Carolina, University Libraries, Rare Books and Special Collections online exhibition, 2008. Web. http://library.sc.edu/spcoll/hist/handwriting/index.html.

Malcolm, Corey. "Understanding the Key West Hurricane of 1846." *Florida Keys Sea Heritage Journal* 20, no. 4 (Summer 2010): 1–16. Print.

Maloney, Walter. *A Sketch of the History of Key West, Florida*. Gainesville: University of Florida Press, 1968. (Reprint of 1876 original text).

Manning, Carol S. *The Female Tradition in Southern Literature*. Champaign: University of Illinois Press, 1993. Print.

Miller, Emily. "Micanopy Loses an Icon in Bookseller O. J. Briskey." *Gainesville Sun*. February 1, 2014. https://www.gainesville.com/article/LK/20140201/News/604131868/GS.

Murray, Judith Sargent. "On the Equality of the Sexes." In *Selected Writings of Judith Sargent Murray*, ed. Judith Sargent Murray and Sharon M. Harris, 3–14. Oxford: Oxford University Press, 1995. *EBSCOhost*: https://search.ebscohost.com/login.aspx?direct=true&AuthType=shib&db=nlebk&AN=143816&site=eds-live&scope=site.

Mott, Lucretia. *Discourse on Woman*. Philadelphia, 1850. *Sabin Americana*. Gale, Cengage Learning. Florida Southern College. Accessed January 6, 2017: http://galenet.galegroup.com/servlet/Sabin?af=RN&ae=CY107613904&srchtp=a&ste=14.

Oberholtzer, Ellis Paxon. *The Literary History of Philadelphia*. George W. Jacobs & Company, 1906. Print.

OED Online. Oxford: Oxford University Press, June 2022. www.oed.com.

Oettermann, Stephen. *The Panorama: History of a Mass Medium*. Translated by Deborah Lucas Schneider. New Nork: Zone Books, 1997. Print.

Ogle, Maureen. *Key West: History of an Island of Dreams*. Gainesville: University Press of Florida, 2003. Print.

O'Sullivan, Maurice. "Interpreting Florida: Its Nineteenth-Century Literary Heritage." *Florida Historical Quarterly* 94, no. 3 (Winter 2016): 320–65. Print.

O'Sullivan, Maurice, and Jack C. Lane. *The Florida Reader: Visions of Paradise from 1530 to the Present*. Sarasota, Fla.: Pineapple Press, 1991. Print.

Patrick, Rembert, ed. "William Adee Whitehead's Description of Key West." *Tequesta* 12 (1952): 61–74. Print.

Perry, Carolyn, and Mary Louise Weaks. *The History of Southern Women's Literature*. Baton Rouge: Louisiana State University Press, 2002. Print.

Peters, Thelma. "William Adee Whitehead's Reminiscences of Key West." *Tequesta* 25 (1965): 3–42. Print.

Policy, Carole. "Defending the Middle Florida Plantation: Caroline Hentz's Jackson County in *Marcus Warland, Or the Long Moss Spring*." *Florida Studies: Proceedings of the 2005 Annual Meeting of the Florida College English Association* 1 (2006): 81–89. Print.

Ransom, James Birchett. *Osceola, or, Fact and Fiction: A Tale of the Seminole War*. Harper, 1838. *Sabin Americana: History of the Americas, 1500–1926*. Accessed July 17, 2022: link.gale.com/apps/doc/CY0102102805/SABN?u=lake33936&sid=bookmark-SABN&xid=b3305990&pg=2.

Roberson, Susan L. *Antebellum American Women Writers and the Road: American Mobilities*. England, U.K.: Routledge, 2012. Print.

Roberts, Mary Louise. "True Womanhood Revisited." *Journal of Women's History* 14, no. 1 (Spring 2002): 150–55. *EBSCOhost*. http://ezproxy.flsouthern.edu:2048/login?url=http://search.ebscohost.com/login.aspx?direct=true&AuthType=ip,uid&db=a9h&AN=6479854.

Robertson, Mary D. "Antebellum Journals and Collections of Letters." In *The History of Southern Women's Literature*, ed. Carolyn Perry and Mary Louise Weaks. Baton Rouge: Louisiana State University Press, 2002.

Rosowski, Susan J. "The Novel of Awakening." In *The Voyage In: Fictions of Female Development*, 49–60. Print.

Scott, Kenneth, and Charles Walker. "The City of Wreckers: Two Key West Letters of 1838." *Florida Historical Quarterly* 25, no. 2 (October 1946): 191–201. Print.

Smith, Karen Manners. "The Novel." In *The History of Southern Women's Literature*, ed. Carolyn Perry and Mary Louise Weaks, 148–58. Baton Rouge: Louisiana State University Press, 2002.

Smith, Reverend Michael. *The Lost Virgin of the South*. 2nd ed. 1833. Google Books. https://www.google.com/books/edition/The_Lost_Virgin_of_the_South/K6hJDKexle4C?hl=en&gbpv=1&dq=The+Lost+Virgin+of+the+South&pg=RA1-PA1&printsec=frontcover.

Spencer, H. C. *Spencerian Key to Practical Penmanship*. New York: Ivison, Phinney, Blakeman & Co., 1866. Print.

Stanton, Elizabeth Cady, et al. *Elizabeth Cady Stanton*. New York: Arno, 1969. Print.

Tebeau, Charlton W. *A History of Florida*. Miami, Fla.: University of Miami Press, 1971. Print.

Tomlinson, Alan, dir. and ed. "Key West Wreckers." WLRN, Miami. Documentary Film. https://www.pbs.org/video/wlrn-history-key-west-wreckers/.

Tompkins, Jane. *Sensational Designs: The Cultural Work of American Fiction, 1790–1860*. Oxford: Oxford University Press, 1986. *EBSCOhost,* search.ebscohost.com/login.aspx?direct=true&AuthType=shib&db=nlebk&AN=143647&scope=site.

Warren, Joyce W. *The (Other) American Traditions: Nineteenth-century Women Writers*. New Brunswick, N.J.: Rutgers University Press, 1993. Online.

Weaks, Mary Louise. "The Antebellum and Bellum South (Beginnings to 1865): Introduction to Part I." In *The History of Southern Women's Literature*, ed. Carolyn Perry and Mary Louise Weaks, 7–16. Baton Rouge: Louisiana State University Press, 2002. Print.

———. "Gender Issues in the Old South." In *The History of Southern Women's Literature*, ed. Carolyn Perry and Mary Louise Weaks, 32–47. Baton Rouge: Louisiana State University Press, 2002. Print.

Wells, Jonathan Daniel. *Women Writers and Journalists in the Nineteenth-Century South*. Cambridge: Cambridge University Press, 2011. Online.

Welter, Barbara. "The Cult of True Womanhood: 1820–1860." *American Quarterly* 18, no. 2, Part 1 (Summer 1966): 151–74. Accessed June 22, 2017: http://www.jstor.org/stable/2711179.

"What I Saw at Key West." (Tallahassee) *Florida Sentinel,* May 11, 1852. Florida Digital Newspaper Library. https://newspapers.uflib.ufl.edu/UF00079923/00694/zoom/2.

Wollstonecraft, Mary. *A Vindication of the Rights of Woman* (1792). Ed. Eileen Hunt Botting. New Haven, Conn.: Yale University Press, 2014. Print.

III. Photographs

Florida Memory. "Early Views of Key West." *Floridiana,* 2013. Accessed June 8, 2022: https://www.floridamemory.com/items/show/295141.

Engraving of Wreckers at Work. Circa 1858. State Archives of Florida, Florida Memory. Accessed June 8, 2022: https://www.floridamemory.com/items/show/25796.

All reproductions of portraits of Aldrich-Anderson-Brown family members are used with permission of Jane Gill, Raymond Gill, and Elizabeth Traynor.

INDEX

Page numbers in *italics* refer to illustrations.

Aldrich, Corinna. *See* Brown (Aldrich), Corinna
Aldrich, Dr. Edward Sherman: marriage to Corinna Brown, 6; moves to Jacksonville, 6; moves to Key West, 12; moves to Macon (Georgia), 6; moves to Newnansville, 8; moves to San Francisco, 13; moves to St. Mary's (Georgia), 6
Aldrich-Anderson-Brown papers (Anderson-Brown papers), 1, 86–88, 93n5
Anderson, Corinna Georgia ("Georgia"), 8, *40*, 89–92
Anderson, Edward Willoughby, 8, 14, 87–88
Anderson, Ellen. *See* Brown (Anderson), Ellen Maria
Anderson, Ellen Mannevillette ("Villette"), 8, *41*, 87, 91
Anderson, James Willoughby ("Will"), *7*, 7, 12
Antebellum literary culture: the bildungsroman, 25–28, 37nn14–15; domestic novels, 24–25; the novel of awakening, 27–28; publishing and technology, 20–21; travel literature, 21–22; realism, 23; sentimentalism, 23–24, 37n; women writers, 22–28
Audubon, James N., 38n27

Bridgeport, Conn., 13
Briskey, O. J., 89, 94n11
Brown, Adelaide, 6
Brown, Charles Burroughs, 2, 4–5, 6
Brown (Aldrich), Corinna, *xiv*; birth, 2; death of, 14, 87; describes Seminole attacks, 7; and first arrival in Florida, 6; marriage to Edward Aldrich, 6; moves to Jacksonville, 6; moves to Key West, 12; moves to Macon (Georgia), 6; moves to Newnansville 8; moves to New York City, 13; moves to St. Mary's (Georgia), 6; poor health, 13; writings of, 1, 3–5, 9
Brown, Rev. David, 11, 12
Brown (Anderson), Ellen Maria, *xiv*; birth, 2; concern with education, 10; concern with women's marital role, 19; death of, 87; and first arrival in Florida, 6; lives in Philadelphia, 4–5; marries Lt. James Willoughby Anderson, 8; moves to Key West, 12; moves to New York City, 89; writing career and writings of, 1, 3–5, 9, 13, 14, *41*
Brown, Elihu Dearing, 2, 17
Brown, Elizabeth Dearing, 2
Brown, George Long: birth, 2; death of, 14, 86; wedding, 13
Brown, Mannevillette Elihu Dearing, *3*; birth, 2; death of, 88, 91; moves to Ithaca, NY, 9; moves to Paris, France, 6; writes novel with sisters, 3–4
Bruce, Betty, 93n10

Condit, Cyrus Parkhurst, 32–33
Cooper, James Fenimore, 34–35
Cowper, William, 121
Creek tribe, 8
Curtis, George William, 15. *See also Potiphar Papers, The*
Cusick, Dr. James, 85

Dearing, Ann, 2, 6
Dearing, Delia (Dorothy). *See* Hall, Delia (Dorothy) Dearing
Dearing, Mary, 2, 6
Denham, Dr. James M., 36n1, 85–86

Farnum, J. Egbert, 14
Florida: literary tradition of, 30–35; women's perspective in literature of, 29
Fox (privateering vessel), 17

Gill, Jane Meyer, 93n8
Gill, Raymond, 93n8
"The Grumble Family," 85
Goolsby, Lewis, 86, 88

Hall, Delia (Dorothy) Dearing, 6
Hall, Dr. James, 6, 9
Hentz, Caroline Lee, 32
Hoffman, Dr. Charles A., 86, 88

Jacksonville, 6, 7
Jacksonville *Courier,* 11

Key West: Aldrich family in, 8; diverse population of, 83n15; engraving of, *40;* fiction about, 29–35; hurricane of 1846, 84nn27,28; lighthouse, 83n19; mosquitoes, 15; name of, 82n11; pencil sketch of, 35; photograph of, *39;* shipwreck salvaging industry in, 16–18, 36n7

La Coe, Norman (Norm), 86, 88–89, 92n4, 93n7, 93n10
Levy, David. *See* Yulee, David Levy

Mandarin, 6, 7
Mexican War, 8
Meyer, Mary Gedner, 93n9
Mineral Springs, 6

Nank, Christopher, 94n15
New York City, 13
"Novel in a Nut-Shell, A," 13, 85, 95–116
Newnansville, 8

P. K. Yonge Library, 1, 85, 91
Pensacola: Aldrich family in, 8
Postal system, 37n10
Potiphar Papers, The, 15, 83n16, 90
Philadelphia, 2, 3–4, 4–5
Portsmouth, New Hampshire, 2, 5

Second Seminole War, 7
Seminole tribe, 6–8, 36n3
Sketches of Life During the Second Seminole War, 9, 29
Slavery, 82n9
Steamboat travel, 84n22, 84n24
St. Augustine, 3, 6
Storm, The: compared to *A Trip to Florida for Health and Sport,* 32–33; concern with women's societal roles, 19–20; feminism in, 19–20; illustrations for, 89–92; likely composition of, 15; manuscript of, *42,* 85–89; narrator of, 15–17, 31; shipwreck salvaging in, 17–18
Sullivan, Mannevillette, 93nn5,6

Traynor, John, Jr., 86, 88–89, 93nn5,7
Traynor, Elizabeth, 91–92, 93n9
Traynor, Elizabeth ("Betsy"), 88, 93n8

United States Military Academy, 28

Wollstonecraft, Mary, 36–37n9

Yulee, David Levy, 7

Keith L. Huneycutt, professor of English at Florida Southern College, earned his Ph.D. in English from the University of North Carolina at Chapel Hill. Since 1987, he has taught numerous courses at Florida Southern, primarily in European, British, and Florida literature. His publications include various articles on Florida literature, history, and culture and two books coauthored with James M. Denham: *Echoes From a Distant Frontier: The Brown Sisters' Correspondence from Antebellum Florida* and *The Letters of George Long Brown: A Yankee Merchant on America's Southernmost Antebellum Frontier.* A former president of the Florida College English Association, he was awarded that organization's Distinguished Colleague Award in 2011. He currently serves on the board of trustees for the Marjorie Kinnan Rawlings Society and as the associate editor for *The Marjorie Kinnan Rawlings Journal of Florida Literature.*

Printed in the United States
by Baker & Taylor Publisher Services